SHADOW PANDEMIC

BOOK 1 OF SHADOW TRILOGY

H.G. AHEDI

First edition published in 2021
Copyright © H.G Ahedi 2021

ISBN: 9780648779896 (eBook)
ISBN: 9780645105520 (Print)
Book cover concept by H.G. Ahedi
Book cover designed Rebecca covers (fiver.com)

CONTENTS

"Hell is empty and all the devils are here."

William Shakespeare

1

THE BEGINNING OF THE END

15th February 2020 (Present day)
Nightridge

Darkness loomed as the purple clouds hovered on the horizon. A thick layer of fog descended on the small town of Nightridge, blanketing the dark trees in utter silence.

Here, far away from the heart of town, four shadows lurked in the woods. At a distance, a subtle whirring began. As it drew closer, a bright light cut through the darkness, and the whirring became louder. The fog quickly dissipated as a helicopter descended, throwing dust in every direction.

The lights almost blinded Dr. William Sterling. He turned to notice the bright light near the town center.

It had started.

William Sterling glanced at Sheriff Norris Cunningham, who was armed and ready. To Sheriff's left was Deputy Kyle Torres. Fredrick Walsh stood away from the trio. William got the feeling that Fredrick was not only afraid of the villagers but also of the men with him. He kept glancing nervously in the forest's direction.

Yes, they might attack at any time, he thought

William couldn't believe it. A few weeks ago, everything was normal, whatever 'normal' meant during the Pandemic. Norris was a cop he had known for several years. He was steady, strong, and someone he trusted. Kyle was a young deputy who was loyal to the sheriff and community. Fredrick was a county coroner with whom William had spent a lot of time during the last two weeks. He was young, anxious, and unpredictable. They were able men, but could they do this? He didn't know.

They waited as the container settled on the back of the truck with a loud thud. The ropes were released and fell on the top of the container. The helicopter's passenger door opened, and a figure jumped on the container. It waved towards the pilot. Soon the helicopter gained altitude and flew away. The figure looked around and jumped to the ground.

William was thrilled to see the detective. "Tom!"

They hugged each other, and William felt a great sense of relief.

"You, okay?" Detective Tom Nash of the NYPD asked as they parted.

"Yes. Yes!" William replied.

"Who else is coming?" Norris inquired.

Tom shook his head in dismay and replied, "No one!"

William's heart sank.

"What?! This is an emergency... people are dying!" Norris yelled.

"I know, Sheriff, they didn't believe me! I tried. They don't believe me. They think the pandemic is the bigger problem right now!" replied Tom.

Everyone glanced at each other. The pandemic was a priority—there was no doubt about that in William's mind, but they could have sent some help. "We can't do this alone!" he said.

A loud blast echoed. An enormous ball of fire hurtled toward the sky.

"Oh my god," Norris muttered.

The five men glanced at each other in horror.

"Well, I hope this works," Tom muttered.

"We have to make it work," said Norris. He turned to the group. "You know what to do. Remember, you hesitate, you die."

2

LIFE IS FRAGILE

3rd February 2020
Nightridge

Sheriff Norris Cunningham sat on the porch of his twenty-year-old house. The one-story dwelling sat amid a green yard lined by a white picket fence. It was a blissful morning, and he tried his best to savor it. His coffee was turning cold, and he felt his fingers freezing, but he didn't leave the porch. The sky was striking blue, the wind gentle and the winter sun perched above his neighbor's roof. He tried to soak the warmth of the winter sun. In this crazy world, a little peace was always welcome. It was hard, and his mind kept racing, wondering and worrying about the future. The past few months had been tough for him—just like every other human being on the planet.

Nightridge, the village he was born in, was silent. Even

the birds weren't singing. One would say villages are often quiet, but he didn't like this unsettling stillness. He sensed as if something was going to happen. Something perhaps worse than the pandemic.

He rubbed his face, feeling the scrub of his beard and brushing his thick mustache. Nearing his fifties, Norris resembled a cowboy who had just stepped out of an old western movie. He was tall, with a stern face and broad shoulders.

Since he was a boy, he knew he wanted to be in law enforcement. After serving his country in the war, he had a long successful career as an officer. Being in this field wasn't easy, but it came naturally to him. However, the past few months felt like a test. Life was pushing him to the limits.

A thought crept into his mind. *Why not just end it all? There is nothing to live for.*

He refused to give in because it was not only him who was suffering. Everyone was in the same situation. People were wary, scared of this unseen virus that mutated and suffocated its victim to death. There was no cure, not yet. The country was divided. While the rich could survive the lockdown, others struggled to pay off their debts and mortgages because of loss of jobs.

As the sheriff of Nightridge, he had to enforce the lockdown procedures. Making masks and sanitizers compulsory, shutting down public places and asking people to stay indoors was hard. But compared to the city, Nightridge was in a better position. Social distancing was easy. The overall result was good, and the number of cases had dropped, but over time the villagers were becoming distressed.

Every day he received complaints from wives suspecting husbands of trying to kill them and husbands reporting that their food was being poisoned. Younger people were harder to control and often snuck out of the houses to wander into the wilderness. This week alone, his deputies had arrested three teenagers.

Norris sipped his coffee and tried to loosen up. He was getting tired, annoyed, and no longer thought it was worth it. He was a sheriff, not a babysitter. The rules were simple—protect yourself, stay indoors. Why couldn't people follow simple rules?

He wanted to quit his job, but then what would he do? He might help his daughter and spend time with his granddaughter. A wave of grief overpowered him. He saw cremation jars. Trying to fight this feeling of anguish, he took another sip of the cold coffee.

Don't think about it... you tried your best. You couldn't be there. You didn't have a choice. No choice!

He wiped away his tears.

3

DOOMSDAY

15th February 2020
(Present day)

W illiam understood the plan. It was his idea, and it was all they had. He wished someone would come up with a better one. A sensible one. It was not to be.

"Here," Tom said, handing over a black laptop briefcase.

Without a word, William took it and hung it over his shoulder. They had to guard it with their lives. It was the key to save them. Save everyone.

"Take the container back to the village," said Norris.

"I am not going back there!" cried out Fredrick.

William pitied him. Fredrick was young, fresh out of the university, and a trainee coroner. He wasn't ready for this. William wanted to say more and give him some comfort, but he failed.

"We have no choice," said Norris.

Fredrick cringed.

"We'll go to the bridge, and you head towards the village," said Norris.

"Okay. Remember, whatever happens, we can't let them leave," William said.

"I'll make sure of that," answered Norris.

"I think we should leave," yelled Fredrick. "Call the pilot... I want to leave! Now! I can't stay... I can't do this!"

Norris grabbed him. "We need you. The villagers need you."

"No, they don't! It's not worth it!"

"Fredrick..." said Norris.

"We are going to die. We are all going to die! They are going to kill us!"

The men fell silent. All of them knew the consequences.

"Go!" ordered Norris.

"I'll stay with you," William said to Fredrick. "We'll be fine. You have to trust me."

Tom climbed into the truck and got behind the wheel. William and Fredrick joined him. With a heavy heart, William watched the sheriff's truck drive down the misty highway. He faced Tom and asked, "How did you get permission to leave?"

Tom gazed at him. "How long have you known me? I don't ask for permission."

· · ·

The truck began moving down the road. With fear in his eyes, William gawked at the unlit road ahead. His heart was pounding in his chest. He turned to see the black container from the truck's back window. He shut his eyes.

Why didn't I figure this out sooner? It's all on me. It's my fault. I could have stopped this. He thought.

4

THE CITY OF FEARS

3rd February 2020
New York City

The smog was so thick that the skyline wasn't visible. William sipped his coffee, not even enjoying the taste. Coffee at 7 am. It was a habit, just like brushing his teeth. The city that never sleeps was under lockdown due to the drastic turn of events that no one saw coming. It was like living in a nightmare. He felt like a character in an apocalypse movie. Unfortunately, this movie never seemed to end.

The pandemic had shown him the true face of brutality, and he thought he was losing his mind and everything else. He was a medical examiner who worked at the city morgue. Death was something he dealt with every day, but this was more terrifying than anything he had ever experienced.

When the pandemic struck, William and several of his colleagues volunteered to help at the hospital. But as the death toll rose, he thought he would have been better off at the morgue. It was preferable because people were already dead. At the hospital, he struggled to save lives he knew he couldn't. He had to watch mothers losing children and husbands losing wives. Most of all, people died alone, without saying goodbye to their loved ones. They were dying in the dark, behind curtains surrounded by faceless men and women who were as helpless as the patients themselves.

He shrugged his shoulders. Doctors always have to face the fear of losing a patient, but his generation had never experienced a pandemic. And if he thought the morgue was going to be any different, he was wrong. He had been there yesterday, and it was worse. He was paralyzed. Powerless. Scared. William wanted things to go back to normal. If there was such a thing. But the truth was, there was no running away from reality.

The bathroom door opened, and Joan stepped out in a shirt. He admired her long, beautiful legs as she came to stand beside him. He put his arm around her, and they embraced each other.

Joan was an athletic woman, around his height, with brown, almond-shaped eyes. A homicide detective with the NYPD, Joan was fighting her own demons, just like him. He feared for her safety. In this crazy world, he didn't want her out in the streets and was grateful for the lockdown. She sometimes went out on patrols, but it was with her partner, Detective Tom Nash. Her partners presence with her gave William a lot of comfort.

The lockdown had other effects. They had been dating for couple of years, and neither of them ever thought about moving in together. The pandemic changed that. Joan had planned to stay for a few days, but it had turned into weeks. Cohabitating had its pros and cons. He could see skeletons in her closet and she could see his. And there were too many of them.

He turned to the window and tried to see through the fog. It appeared as if he was in a parallel universe. His world had turned upside down, and in this cruel universe, he was separated from his friends and family.

"I miss you guys," he whispered.

5

RAGING FIRE

15th February 2020 (Present day)
Highway

Norris's palms were sweating. He was breathless, and a part of him wished to stop the car, weep and have a meltdown. He had the choice to walk into the woods and let the world destroy itself. Leave and never look back. However, it wasn't that simple. This was his world. His village. His home. He had too much to lose. Most of his family was gone; and he was trying to salvage what remained of his life.

Norris shook his head. Weakness was not something he liked to show, especially to a junior officer. Kyle was a great guy, almost the same age as his own son. He was dedicated to his work, family and the village. For Norris, he was near perfect. A happy-go-lucky young man, an efficient worker who never fretted about any task assigned to him.

Norris tried to focus on driving. Thick forest dominated the road on both sides and he peered into the woods, but saw nothing. A clicking noise almost made him jump. It was Kyle loading his shotgun. His hands shook as he put bullets in the barrel.

"No one is coming to help us," he muttered, picking up his handgun and checking the clip.

"It will be okay. We will hold the fort. Tom was unsuccessful, but I know Cranston will come through. He always does."

Norris thought he was lying. What could Cranston do? He wasn't even in the country, but Norris wanted to believe in something. He wanted to hope. It was the only thing he had.

He turned off the headlights and slowed down as they reached near the sheriff's office.

"Remember, we remain out of sight. Do not make a noise. Do you understand?"

Kyle nodded.

The truck came to a standstill; the lights turned off, and it became dead silent. Thick mist surrounded them and the streetlights appeared like dim bulbs hanging in the sky. The fog whisked along with the wind, and the temperature dropped. Norris tried to look past the mist, but saw nothing. It was too dense. He knew they were out there. Waiting. Hungrier than ever. Raging and full of anger.

Highway

The truck cut through the thick fog on the wet road. It was slower and louder than the sheriff's vehicle, and the heater wasn't keeping them warm.

William checked his handgun for bullets. "Tom, how many bullets do you have?" he asked.

"Three rounds."

"You should have brought more guns."

"Are you nuts? What if they kill us and take them? Just think, how many more innocent people would die?"

William frowned, but he understood. Fredrick shivered in the middle, and William wished he could say something to calm him down. But every man had to face their demons tonight, including himself. He wished they would leave this place alive. Glancing back at the container, he checked his mobile for messages. There were none. That was not a good sign.

6

LOCK DOWN MURDER

3rd February 2020
Meadow Cottage

Norris looked at the omelet. It was alright, his wife was an excellent cook and he did his best. It was fine as long as it was edible.

Oh, dear Martha, he thought

Martha was long gone, but her memories were fresh in his mind. He thought of Lucy, his only daughter and his granddaughter, who lived in Maryland. Before the pandemic, he traveled once a month to see her, but now that was impossible.

Playing with his granddaughter, holding her in his arms, was something he missed. The ache in his heart returned, and he saw the cremation jars again. He wiped his tears as the memories haunted him. Pushing those thoughts away, he got ready to eat breakfast. The phone rang.

"Oh, what is it this time?" he muttered.

The last call was from a schoolteacher. He thought the school's principal was evil and had sold his soul to the devil. It was a bizarre conversation, but it wasn't the first absurd allegation he had heard since the lockdown.

"Yes," he said as he answered the phone.

"Chief," said Deputy Hector Mathews nervously.

"Yes, Hector, what is it?"

"Chief, I think you should come down to Nicholas's place."

"Why?"

Before he spoke, Hector took a sharp breath in. "There has been a murder."

Norris stared in disbelief at the wall. "I'll be there in fifteen minutes," he replied and hung up.

His heart was beating fast as he grabbed his hat and winter coat and rushed out of the door. His truck was parked right beside the gates. He pushed the gates open, got behind the wheel, and drove off.

The streets were empty, covered by the thick shades of trees on both sides. The road was smooth as Norris drove past several houses. He saw a few villagers outside working in their yards.

Norris drove by Billy's house, surrounded by a sizeable garden. Six motorcycles stood in the front of the open garage. Billy and three of his men were fixing motorcycles, while two others were sitting on boxes, smoking. Rowdy, outlaws, and men without honor, merit or jobs. Norris wasn't happy they were in the village. But like everyone, they couldn't travel. Otherwise, like every year, Billy and his friends would hang around for a couple of weeks and then ride away. The lockdown had changed many things.

Norris stopped his truck in front of a double-story house. The air was cold and misty. He stepped out of the truck and walked toward the door. A green lawn surrounded the house, lined with beautiful lilies. A water fountain stood in the garden's heart.

Deputy Hector Mathews stood alongside the porch as paramedics attended to the man on the stretcher. Norris's heart jumped a beat; it was Nicholas Murphy. He removed his hat, dropped to his knees, and looked at his old friend. They went to school and college together. Then Norris decided to serve his country, and Nicholas took control of his father's timber factory.

The paramedic was attending to the older chap. Lacerations on his hands appeared like defense wounds. His breathing was shallow, and as he turned to Norris, his eyes were full of confusion and terror.

"Daisy… Daisy…" Nicholas whispered.

Norris stood up and placed his hand on his friend's shoulder.

"We need to take him to the hospital," said the paramedic.

Norris nodded and turned to Hector. "What happened?"

Hector said nothing and gestured him to go inside the house.

Norris cautiously stepped into the house. Everything had been tossed and torn apart. Blood splatter smudged the walls. In the middle lay a fragile body. As he neared it, he gasped. It was Daisy, Nicholas's fifteen-year-old daughter. His heart filled with anguish. The skin around her eyes was burned, and the rest of the skin was peeling away as if melting.

"What the hell?" he uttered.

"I know."

"What did Nicholas say?"

"Chief, he is in shock. The man can hardly breathe."

"You mean she did that to him?"

"It appears that she attacked him, and then she collapsed and stopped breathing."

"What?" He glanced back at the corpse. "What about Mary Murphy?"

The deputy grimly turned toward the kitchen.

Feeling a lump in his throat, Norris walked into the kitchen. He shut his eyes upon seeing Mary Murphy.

"No. No," he muttered.

There was blood on her blouse, and he gently pulled the tip of the blouse and noted the bullet hole in her chest. He hung his head. He had known Mary all his life. Her slender face was white as a ghost, and her eyes remained open, filled with terror. A gun laid near the dining table chair.

"What happened here?" Norris muttered.

"Well, it looks like the daughter shot the mother and then attacked the father," replied Hector.

Norris was stumped. Why would Mary's daughter do this to her? She was the loveliest woman in town—a teacher, a giver who survived cancer only to be shot by her own blood.

Coroner Fredrick Walsh arrived with the coroner's bag in his hand. A talented young man who had temporarily inherited the job from an experienced coroner who had died of old age.

Norris saw the hesitation in Fredrick's eyes.

The timid man in his thirties adjusted his heavy glasses. His curly hair was short, and he stood hunched forward, keenly observing the body.

Norris didn't know if he was hesitant about approaching the corpse or if he was simply thinking.

Fredrick had dealt with several victims of the COVID-19 virus in the past few months, but a murder was something new. Without warning, Fredrick reached for his bag and took out a camera with a big lens. He eyed Norris, who got the hint, and signaled his men to leave.

Outside, Norris found a chair on the porch and sat down, feeling dejected. Hector appeared upset, made an excuse, and left. It was okay. Norris didn't need him right now. The two paramedics assigned to help transfer the body waited for the coroner to finish.

The door opened and Fredrick stepped out. The paramedics entered the house to take the bodies to the morgue. Norris peeped inside to see several yellow tags. The paramedics carried the two bodies to the black van. Fredrick and Norris exchanged confused glances. Norris thought he was about to say something, but he suddenly bowed and walked toward the van.

Interesting guy, thought Norris.

As soon as the black van left, a gray Mercedes stopped in front of the gate. Mayor Henry Rogers stepped out. Henry was older than Norris. He walked with a bit of a limp and tried to hide his overweight body by wrapping his coat around himself. The mayor lived in a sizable house in the village with his wife Charlotte.

Norris was surprised. He hadn't seen the mayor for ages. Not since the pandemic was declared. Henry communicated and threw orders from the safety of his house, which some might think was a good idea. His overall support towards the villagers was next to none.

Norris believed Henry was a coward. Then he reconsidered this thought. It was not the time to judge people. Henry had suffered, just like everyone else.

"Sheriff," Henry said coldly.

"Mr. Mayor," he replied with equal distaste.

"It's sad business."

Norris could say nothing but nod. Henry had been aloof and bitter with everyone, including himself. It had started with his son Jeffery passing away. Another victim of the pandemic.

"What do you think happened?" Henry asked.

"Before dying, Daisy shot her mother, and attacked her father. We do not know why."

Henry nodded. "Yes. Sometimes, bad things happen."

"How are you?" Norris asked.

"I am fine. I am fine."

Norris tried to smile.

"Let me know what you find. And, Sheriff, try to keep the press away from this one."

"I don't think the press would be a problem. They don't care about little town murders."

Henry looked unsure. "Just try to get this wrapped up soon, okay?"

"I'll do what is necessary," he answered.

Henry nodded, turned towards his car.

Suddenly Norris remembered he hadn't seen Henry's wife for a while. "Say hello to Charlotte!"

Henry waved without looking back.

DO NOT OPEN

15th February 2020 (Present day)
Nightridge

The houses burned, and fires erupted, throwing flames in every direction. Norris waited for his chance. It was dark except for the yellow glow cast by the fire raging at a distance. He stood up and began moving. Kyle was right behind him as they approached the small structure. He never thought he would have to sneak into his own office. He reached the half-broken door and looked around. They were all alone. He quickly stepped in.

Inside it was dark, and he dared not to switch on the light. Sound and light appeared to draw their attention. They had stayed low and out of sight. It was vital if he wanted their plan to succeed. Sweat dripped from his forehead as his eyes adjusted to the darkness. They had trashed the office. Desks were flipped over, and chairs were broken. Paper and files were scattered all over the floor. Ugly graffiti covered the walls.

In the dim light, he read the words. "Fuck the law!"

The words on the other wall were more disturbing.

"Kill everyone. Burn the world."

His heart pounded in his chest, and he pushed his thoughts aside as he rushed toward the end of the hall and approached one of the locked doors. No one had broken into it. He unlocked it and closed the door behind them. Switching on the light in the windowless room, he glared at the boxes.

"Where is it?"

"It should be here," replied Kyle, frantically searching.

Fearing that their time was running out, they hurriedly began looking.

"Got it," Kyle said, moving the boxes away. He slowly picked it up and placed it in a corner. Norris recognized the box. They had to hide it so it wouldn't be easily accessible. No one knew about it except him and Kyle. With a heavy heart, he read the label.

DANGER EXPLOSIVES
PROCEED WITH EXTREME CAUTION
HANDLE WITH CARE

Nightridge

The truck halted, and the trio felt imminent danger. They were only a mile away from their destination. The situation was dangerous. Volatile. They looked at each other. Tom turned off the headlights, and they sat in silence.

William's phone buzzed; he had received a text message. He quickly read it: *They are here. They are coming. Hide! Hide now!*

"We have to hide," he told Tom.

Tom turned the key, and without turning the head-lights on, he drove the truck into an opened structure. It was an enormous timber factory. Making sure the truck was out of sight, he turned the engine off. They jumped out of the truck and peered out into the gloominess.

William's phone buzzed again. It was another text: *You have ten minutes. Find a secure location. Please. Move. Now!*

William turned to the others. "Let's go!"

BIG MURDER IN SMALL TOWN

3rd February 2020
City Morgue

D r. Sterling stared at the bodies covered with white sheets. There were too many, and he was becoming impatient. Something had to be done. Unfortunately, he was powerless, just a guy who worked in a government building. Except for their families, no one cared what happened to these lifeless figures.

There was no need to figure out the cause of death. Virology already had what they needed. A virus that mutated, destroyed the respiratory system, and killed people. He speculated about why he wasn't infected. Every fifteen days, medical professionals had to undergo testing for COVID-19 and every time he expected his test to be positive. He wondered why he was immune to the virus and donated his blood for DNA testing. Perhaps he was just lucky.

William processed the bodies until sundown, but he believed he was failing at his job. Normally, after his cases were complete, he had the pleasure of returning the victim's bodies to the families and giving them some sort of closure. He rejoiced this part of his job where he would get the opportunity to explain the reason for the death or gather evidence and help catch the killer.

But now, it seemed like he was running a disposal machine. The bodies were not released to the families, so there was no closure, no conversation, or explanations. After informing the families, they burned the corpses as if they meant nothing.

William drove home and felt the surrounding chaos. Every human walking on the sideway appeared like a carrier of death. Why didn't they just stay at home? Everyone had their reasons. Mostly, it was money. People had to eat and pay rent, and most of them depended on their daily wages. With the city almost shutting down, fear of starving to death or losing their livelihood was haunting several citizens. The world was in chaos. Thankfully, there were fewer police on the road, and his medical ID gave him the option of traveling without being questioned by the police.

He unlocked the door to his apartment, and it was silent. A dread took over him. Joan and he hadn't spoken for a while. She tried to talk; he said little. He wasn't sure what was wrong. Was it her or him? He didn't understand. Possibly it was just the way it was in relationships.

He showered and made some dinner. Joan wasn't

home yet. Feeling worried, he picked up the phone and spoke with her. After making sure his girlfriend was safe, William switched the TV on began watching the news. Immediately he felt more depressed. So, he changed the channel and started watching an old comedy movie. When he got bored with TV, he read emails from his friends who were making travel plans for the future. He loved their spirit. They were thinking ahead, making plans. He didn't feel like doing anything. He surfed the internet for a while and came across a blog with the title, "Big Murder in Small Town."

The title piqued his interest. Murder was his thing. The article described about an incident where a man was admitted to the hospital after trying to control his hysterical daughter, who had shot her mother. Three words grabbed his attention: the peeling body.

That's interesting, he thought.

9

BEST PLACE TO HIDE

15th February 2020 (Present day)
Sheriff's Office

Norris used his knife and carefully open the box. He sensed Kyle's discomfort. He cautiously opened and viewed the contents. Piles of C4 were carefully enclosed in protective packing material. He began transferring them into a duffle bag and zipped it. Kyle handed them a remote detonator, and Norris carefully placed them in a smaller bag.

Once they were ready, the men turned the lights off and stepped out. It was silent. Maybe that was a good thing. Maybe it wasn't. Norris tiptoed through the hall and sneaked out the window. For a moment, he felt like he was a teenager again, slipping out of the house in the middle of the night. Those days were long gone.

The darkness and the fog gave the men the perfect

cover. They appeared like two vague figures who appeared and disappeared in the darkness. Norris was glad to find his truck untouched. Kyle placed the bags on the backseat and jumped in. A loud scream echoed in the night. The men froze.

Nightridge

The mist wasn't helping; William stumbled for the third time and almost fell on his face. He sulked. He was supposed to be quiet, but he was not doing a good job. Noise attracted them, and he and his friends had to avoid being discovered. It was dark, and he was in unknown territory. They kept moving through the woods. His ankle throbbed with stabs of pain, and he worried he'd sprained it. He came to a sudden stop when they neared a structure. The two other men slowed down, huffing.

"Why are we stopping?" Tom asked.

"We need to be careful," William answered.

They looked ahead at the small cluster of buildings. William slowly kneeled and waited, not wanting to risk anyone seeing them. That meant their death, or worse. The forest was quiet, and even the wildlife had fled as if sensing the danger. They heard a soft rustle.

"Don't make a sound," whispered William.

The three men huddled together as the shadows moved through the forest. Vague, dark, and dangerous. They eventually melted into the woods. The thick fog lifted for a second, and William saw their destination. It was just nine yards away.

"Okay, let's go."

William was the first to move, followed by Tom and Fredrick. They ran over the gravel. A crackling noise reverberated. William realized his mistake. He looked around and saw no one. As soon as they entered the structure, he locked the door behind him.

Tom armed himself. "Who lives here?"

"No one," Fredrick answered.

William turned to notice Tom's startled face. He followed his gaze and looked at the panel.

"This is a fucking morgue," Tom cried out.

"Shush," William said.

William pushed the others down the hall and opened a steel door. They entered a closed space and a strong, pungent smell hit them. William secured the door while Tom stood in front of five steel beds with figures covered in blankets. A small stream of light crept through the two narrow windows near the ceiling. In the gloomy room, he noticed Tom glaring at him.

"This is not good," muttered Fredrick, "This is not good."

"Are you nuts?!" Tom said loudly when William covered the detective's mouth.

"You shouldn't be worried about the dead," whispered William.

A loud thud echoed, and the men looked toward the roof.

10

THE PEELING BODY

4th February 2020
County Morgue

The autopsy room wasn't classy; it didn't need to be. It was composed of two steel tables, cabinets for storing surgical equipment, an old noisy mortuary refrigerator, a washing area, and a long table along the wall.

Norris stood with his hands on his waist. The morgue smelled disgusting and made his stomach twitch. Daisy's body was still melting. Her face had disappeared, and he noticed the underlying muscles and the scratched eyeballs. Outer layers of the muscles of her right hand were visible. Norris regarded the pale-looking coroner. He didn't blame him; the most complicated thing Fredrick had dealt with were bullet holes.

"Well? What have you found?"

"She died of a cardiac failure," Fredrick told him.

"She's too young for that," said Norris.

"Yes. I'm unsure what caused it. Sheriff, I have collected all the evidence…"

A part of Daisy's shoulder skin peeled and fell over the examination table. Fredrick rushed out, and Norris could hear him vomit. He hung his head and wished they had someone else. Fredrick was a temporary Coroner. Norris hoped they would find his replacement soon.

Fredrick returned moments later. "Sorry," he said.

"I understand this is beyond your…" Norris didn't want to sound unprofessional.

"Skillset," Frederick said. "I just got my degree a year ago. I… I don't know what killed her."

Norris smiled. "I understand. You followed the protocol and did what was necessary, right?"

"Yes. I have collected skin, blood, tissue samples, and swabbed her mouth, her nose and her throat. I have also collected the samples of skin, hair and nails. It may not be needed, but I also swabbed her lady parts just to be sure."

"Thank you for being so thorough."

"Ah, before I forget. The mayor called."

"What did he want?"

"He inquired about Daisy and asked what was the best way to… um… dispose of the body."

"I think we should let the father decide that."

The skin on Daisy's ear peeled away.

Frederick closed his eyes.

"Don't worry, I know just the man for the job," Norris replied jovially.

City Morgue

William stood in Dr. Stephen's office and was surprised that his boss had a problem with him going to Nightridge. He had received a call from Sheriff Cunningham asking for his help to solve a murder. It was the most exciting thing that had happened to him this year. However, he couldn't just drop everything and leave. After all, he was an employee.

William's boss's office was not that big, and Dr. Stephen sat between two cabinets. His desk was full of files and papers.

"We are short on staff," he huffed.

"No, you are not. The morgue is running better than the New York Printing Press. Bodies come in, we process them, we cremate them, and send the paperwork to the basement and the families. Certainly, you can continue this process without me for two weeks?"

"We have a pandemic on our hands!"

"About which we can do nothing!!" William shouted. "We can't save lives! We can't even treat our dead properly! It seems like we are just packing them and sending them off into a void. This is insane!"

Dr. Stephen sat back.

"William, look. Everyone is in the same situation. I can't give you special treatment."

William sulked, but then he remembered. "Oh, well... you can just say I am on leave. I have over two weeks' annual leave left."

"No."

"Come on."

Dr. Stephen fell silent. "You think it's an interesting case?" He said, reading through the preliminary report.

"Yeah."

"We have worked with the sheriff before."

"Yes, a few years ago."

"Do you think your assistant Johnathan can cover for you?" Dr Stephen asked, still reading the file.

"Yes. Yes, he can."

Dr. Stephen smiled. "Fine. Fine. Let's make it official."

William raised his eyebrows.

"God knows we could use some good press. A medical examiner helping a county sheriff should be good for everyone. You want to work in this case; everything goes through me. Understand?"

"Fine… I will give my full report when it's over."

Dr. Stephen smiled. "I expect nothing less."

11

RIDING THE TIDE

15th February 2020 (Present day)
Highway

The truck almost skidded, throwing Norris against the door. Kyle grabbed the dashboard; his face was full of terror. Their eyes wandered around, waiting for them to show up. Norris glanced behind. Nothing. He kept driving.

The truck cut through the mist. The highway was bare, silent, wet, and foggy. It was a moonless night, covered with a blanket of stars. The road was barely visible beyond the sharp beams of the headlights. Norris was thankful that it wasn't snowing. He had to be careful. Very careful.

Norris wiped the sweat off his forehead. He thought moving to the countryside would bring him peace. No more murders. No more serial killers, politics and nonsensical crimes. He was so wrong. Crime was like a disease; it followed him everywhere.

A loud rustle distracted him, and he peered into the dark forest. He saw nothing, but he sensed it. They were out there. Something moved. Was it a shadow or a man? He didn't know. His foot lifted from the accelerator, and the truck slowed down.

"Chief, watch out!" Kyle yelled.

A piercing scream echoed, and a dark figure jumped on the truck. Norris almost lost control, but grabbed the steering. A pair of red eyes glared into his soul.

A loud thumping noise on the roof startled them both, and before he could react, Norris swerved, losing grip of the wheel.

Nightridge

The morgue was dark, the only refuge in the village's chaos. Around it appeared as if the entire world had gone mad. Houses were on fire and the roads overran with chaos and shrieks. Clashing noises of smashed windows dominated their surroundings. Children cried in their beds, women wailed in anger, and men bawled.

William shut his eyes and felt Fredrick trembling at his side. His heart wouldn't stop pounding. His thoughts haunted him, reminding him that this was his fault. He was to blame. To his left was Detective Tom Nash, armed and ready. But how could one detective fight against the entire village?

The three men shook in terror as a loud thud sounded. The pounding continued, and their eyes moved upwards.

Someone was on the roof. William's heart drummed faster, and he wiped the sweat dripping down his neck. They heard a loud roar. It sounded like an animal, but it wasn't.

Another blow reverberated. It was the door. William checked his gun in vain, knowing that he didn't have enough bullets. He heard a loud cry, followed by a brash banging. He held the gun tighter and jumped as an ear-piercing scream filled the air. The banging continued. The door could break anytime. William wondered how would he tackle them? A clattering noise resonated on the other side of the wall. As if someone was dragging a heavy metallic object. William realized who it was. The gang that drove around the village carrying axes. He gulped.

I hope they never find us, he thought.

A woman's scream jolted the three men. He wanted to run outside, make sure she was safe, bring her inside. But tonight, that was not an option. He wouldn't dare go out there. Not now, not until they were ready. People were going to get hurt. Many could die, but they had to wait. There was no other way.

12

PARADISE AWAITS

5th February 2020
New York

Williiam threw a shirt in his suitcase as he heard the door close. He brooded. He knew what was coming. With her hands folded, Joan came to stand beside him. He sensed her disapproval.

"So, you are going away," Joan asked with a hint of distaste.

William gulped. "Yes. There is a case in Nightridge, Sheriff Cunningham needs me."

"I see. Do you have to go?"

"Yes."

"I can help."

She could; she was a hell of a cop. However, he wanted some time alone. Away from NYC. Away from her, and he realized she sensed it.

"Well, I think I should go on my own."

She raised her eyebrows. "I see. Did you tell Roumoult?"

And here we go again, he thought.

Joan was always more concerned about what he said to Roumoult. He had this distinct impression that she often compared their relationship with his friendship with a man he had known for most of his life.

"No. Not yet."

"Oh. I thought you told him everything."

William focused on his packing and closed the suitcase. "Joan, I haven't told him. I want to do something else. I am tired, and feel as if I am losing my mind."

She stared at the ground. "It's tough on all of us."

William shut his eyes. "I agree. Look, I am doing what I can to survive and keep sane. Solving this murder might help me cope better. I need to leave."

She smiled and stepped forward. They kissed and held each other.

"Call me if you need anything," she said.

Sometimes he wondered if he was overreacting, overthinking. Joan loved him, and he knew it.

William's blue Hyundai bounced on the rough road. The two hours' drive was worth it. It not only calmed him down, but also helped him get excited about working on a new case. It had been a while since he had worked on a murder investigation.

The road was barren, quiet, and it appeared as if he had left the shadows of the pandemic far behind. The highway curved along the ocean, and the blissful scenery relaxed him. As he drove ahead, he saw green fields on both sides of the road. There was some traffic, but nothing compared to New York. He noticed several houses, old and new. Cows and buffalos were grazing in the farmlands and fields.

After half an hour, he noted the difference in the terrain. Thick forest surrounded him on both sides, and even the sunlight couldn't penetrate the canopy. He passed a board with the word: Nightridge.

He wasn't far away. Soon he came over a bridge. It was old and narrow. He had to stop in order to let a medium-size truck pass. Once he passed over the bridge, William studied the GPS in his car and noticed this bridge was the only connection between the village and the highway. Dense forest, a mountain and a swamp enclosed the other sides of the village. He checked the address and realized he would reach the sheriff's home soon.

Nightridge

Norris glanced at his watch.

Dr. Sterling should be here any minute, he thought.

At first, Norris thought maybe he should book a hotel for the doc, but it was just for a few days. During the pandemic, it was best and probably safer for William to live with him. Norris had space, and it would be good to have some company.

Norris prepared a room for William and made sure he had enough food and supplies. Norris felt, William was easygoing. But he was, after all, a city boy. Norris could be wrong.

He heard a noise that almost sounded like a gunshot. It was a car backfiring. A car entered the premises of his house. It made a loud groaning noise, as if life was being sucked out of it. It backfired twice before it came to a stop beside his truck.

The man who stepped out was all too familiar to him. William looked the same, but Norris thought his French beard needed a good trim, and like everyone, he needed an actual haircut. The doctor was shorter than him, with broad shoulders, dark brown hair and kind brown eyes. Norris suspected he had gained a few kilos since he had last seen him.

"Morning!" said Dr. Sterling.

"Hi there!"

"Good to see you," Norris said.

They shook hands.

"It has been a long time."

"Indeed. How are you doing?" he asked.

"Not too bad," William replied.

Norris nodded, but wasn't convinced. Both men then disappeared into the house.

13

FAMOUS LAST WORDS

15th February 2020 (Present day)
Highway

Norris pushed the car brakes, and the villager on the bonnet of the truck fell. Norris peered, to make sure he hadn't hurt him. A loud scream echoed, and the car window broke. A woman grabbed Kyle by the neck. Norris hit her in the face, and she stumbled backward and fell on the wet road. He glanced behind. From within the fog, he saw shadows.

"This is crazy. They are everywhere! We will never make it!" shouted Kyle.

Norris remained determined. He turned the key, pushed the accelerator. Driving around the man who was about to jump on the truck again, he floored the paddle. The truck took off and the two figures rushed after the vehicle, screaming and cursing.

Norris glanced at Kyle as he touched his bleeding neck. *This is not good. Not good.* Norris thought, glancing at the speedometer. The situation was getting out of hands. They shouldn't make any more stops, no more delays. He glanced up at the rear-view mirror. The figures had vanished from his vision. For now.

County Morgue

The smoke from the fire was visible from the narrow window above them. The dead bodies in the morgue were silent. William felt safer with them than being outside. A loud bang on the door startled the trio. He clamped his mouth shut, knowing the slightest noise would ruin it all.

This better work, he thought.

He turned to his mobile. Three messages from Joan were waiting for an answer. She was worried. William had asked Tom not to tell her about their situation. Tom didn't listen.

Tom had told Joan everything, and now she was texting him. Shadow pandemic was prevailing, and maybe they could stop it. He wasn't certain when or if help would arrive. His plan might fail, and he might die tonight. All he knew was that his phone's battery will die any time. He had to say it, maybe for the last time. He unlocked the phone and typed; *I love you* and sent the message. His eyes met with Tom's.

A deafening scream killed the silence.

14

A FATHER'S STORY

5th February 2020
Meadow Cottage

After making sure William had settled in, Norris made some lunch. Then they drove toward the town center. William admired his surroundings. Everything around him seemed so fresh, clean, and quiet. Norris slowed down the truck, and William saw a man on the sidewalk waving at them. The sheriff stopped the vehicle. A middle-aged man with kind eyes and curly hair smiled at them. William didn't need to ask who it was. The man wore a collar and was carrying a bible.

"Reverend Ronald Benson, good morning," Norris said.

"Morning. How are you today, son?"

"I am good, thanks," Norris replied.

William smiled.

The reverend was older than Norris, slightly over-weight with a long beard. He had large piercing eyes, and demeaner of someone who took his work seriously.

"And you must be the coroner from the big city."

William introduced himself.

"Well, it's nice of you to come to our little village. I tell you; it was just a young girl having a meltdown. We have no trouble here... we are amiable people."

"Oh, I am sure," William replied, smiling.

"Ah, I sense cynicism."

William remained silent.

"I am sure you will find nothing."

William simply nodded.

The men said their goodbyes, and Norris changed the gear and drove toward their destination. "You don't like priests?" he said.

"No, not really," William answered.

The truck stopped in front of a small structure. William stepped out and wasn't impressed with the morgue. It was in an old building made up of large yellow stones.

They entered the building through a green wooden door. As they wandered down the gloomy corridor, they came across a metallic door. He pushed it open and entered the autopsy room.

"Good enough?"

William smirked. "Where is the lab?"

They walked down the corridor and turned left.

William frowned. The lab was inadequate, and he would have to send samples to the City Morgue. They stepped back out to the hallway, and William noticed another door. It led to a X-ray room.

"Sweet," he muttered.

They returned to the autopsy room and opened the freezer. In there was Daisy's body. Half of the face was gone and the facial muscles were exposed. The skin on the hands and the legs was patchy and lacerated in several places. The muscles on the left hand had withered off, and the bones were visible. Freezing the body had given them more time, and he could collect enough samples to complete his job.

"Just up your alley, isn't it?" Norris remarked.

William chuckled.

"I need to speak with her father and other witnesses. I'll see you in the evening."

"No problem."

Norris nodded and left.

Local Hospital

As he parked his truck in front of the hospital, Norris already knew what to expect. A distressed father seeking answers, but he didn't have any.

The two-floored hospital was a simple white structure. The operation theater, ICU, and the reception were on the ground floor. While the above levels were for patients, radiology and other departments.

As Norris walked through the main door, the receptionist nodded toward him. He waved to her and walked past the reception, through the long and white corridor with gray floors and uncomfortable-looking steel chairs. He walked up the stairs and knocked on room 14.

There was no response. He turned the knob, opened the door, and waited. Looking tired and jaded, Nicholas lay quietly, taking up most of the bed. The blanket tried to keep him covered but failed.

"I knew you would come," he said without looking at him.

Norris took a step forward. "I am sorry."

Tears flowed down Nicholas's face. He didn't deserve this. Nicholas was a big-hearted man. For the last twenty years, he had been running the timber company, which employed over fifty percent of the village. The villagers adored and respected him.

Norris remembered how frustrated Nicholas was when he had to close the timber mill because of the pandemic. But this was far worse. His family was dead, gone. Nothing he could say or do would take the pain away.

"How can this happen to me?"

Norris felt a twist in his gut. The question has been asked too many times, and every time, he had the same answer. "Tragedies happen."

Nicholas gradually moved his head, looking him in the eye.

"Are they really gone? Was that for real?"

Norris's eyes dropped to the floor.

Nicholas began sobbing, slowly at first, and then it turned into a loud hysterical scream. Norris was perplexed. He didn't know what to do. The nurses stepped in and tried to calm Nicholas by sedating him. Norris blamed himself. He should have been more careful and gentler while questioning Nicholas. He was an old friend who had lost everything and needed him.

After a few minutes, Nicholas calmed down. Norris thought it was best to stay with him for a while. The man had lost his entire family in one day, and Norris understood his pain.

After you lose someone, the loss leaves a hole in your chest. You feel a dull pain that never goes away, no matter how much one tried. It's like a void in your life. Everything appears worthless. Since losing his son and grandson, Norris often wondered what was the point of his life?

"Sorry." Nicholas spoke finally.

"No. No. It's okay."

"I want to tell you what happened. It's… like a nightmare! I—I don't know…."

"Take it easy."

"Why? Why did she kill her mother? Attack me?"

"That's what we are going to find out. Tell me everything."

"It was just another morning during this frustrating lockdown!" Nicholas shouted, "There was nothing to do. No one to call and no new orders. There is no work! Just nothing! I thought maybe I could get some workers together, and follow the safety guidelines, and at least keep the company running. I was on the phone talking with the unions. After the call, I felt so tired I decided to sleep a bit more. As I dozed off… I felt my poor wife leave the bed. I wish… I wish I would have woken up with her. I could have saved her. I could have saved Daisy… my… baby." Nicholas sat on the bed with eyes wide-open, staring ahead as if imagining his daughter shooting his wife.

"I didn't see it," he continued. "I was too late. Just too late! I heard a loud bang and rushed to the kitchen. Daisy looked odd. Her face was white, her skin was pasty. She looked sick. It was then I saw Mary, lying on the floor. There was blood everywhere. I called her, she didn't move. I… I looked up and saw my daughter pointing a gun at me. I ducked. She fired one bullet, then another. I pleaded with her to stop. Begged her to stop! But she kept shooting. Norris, she kept shooting! I-I don't know what came over her. She listens to me… but that morning she was not Daisy. She kept pulling the trigger!"

Norris nodded.

"I stayed low, and waited. It became silent, and I realized she had run out of bullets. I peaked out, and she charged toward me with a kitchen knife." He wiped his tears with his trembling hands. "I tried to stop her. She attacked me!" he said as he looked at the bandages on his hands. "She tried to kill me. I took the knife away and pushed her. She stumbled. Suddenly she went into a shock! She started shaking…her eyes turned blood red. She coughed out blood… and then collapsed," Nicholas said, weeping. "I don't know what happened. I didn't hurt her; I swear to God. I didn't!"

"Nicholas… I know you didn't attack your daughter. I know you."

Nicholas sobbed. Norris leaned forward and hugged his friend.

County Morgue

William was a bit surprised; Fredrick was thorough. He had stored the body in the freezer and carefully collected all the skin that had peeled off.

William studied the crime scene photos. He assessed the pictures of the mother's death. Mary Murphy was fifty years old, weighed a hundred and sixty-five pounds, had red hair and blue eyes. In the past she had suffered from cancer. Other than that, she had no known medical conditions. The bullet had missed her heart by two centimeters, punctured her lung, and blood had filled it within seconds. Her death was quick. There was no need for an autopsy. The cause of death was clear.

He turned to the small container. In it was the bullet that Fredrick had retrieved from the body. William picked up the murder weapon, a 38-caliber gun manufactured by Sturm Ruger & Co. He opened the gun and noticed the barrel was empty. It was registered to the father who had never used it. All the bullets fired by Daisy had been collected and kept in separate containers.

"They are from the same gun," said Fredrick.

"I know. I just like to be thorough."

He opened the container with the bullet that had taken Mary's life and studied it under a large magnifying glass. He observed four striations, slightly crooked in the middle. Except that there were no other marks. He compared the striation on the bullets that were embedded in the wall. They matched. He didn't want to leave any stone unturned. He prepared the bullets, the shells and the gun to be dispatched for a proper ballistic examination and report. They must find out if this gun was used for any other crimes.

He turned his attention to Daisy. She was under-weight, five feet six inches tall, blonde with blood-shot eyes. He examined the crime scene photos and raised his eyebrows. The skin on her arms, legs and face was withering away. The burnt skin around her eyes was a curious reaction. Was she exposed to something? A toxin? A chemical? A poison?

William went through the evidence collected at the crime scene. Fredrick's preliminary examination did not reveal any stab wounds or needle marks, but there was some bruising on her hands. Fredrick thought it was when the father tried to stop the daughter. All the fingerprints, the blood spatter, proved that the daughter killed the mother and attacked the father. He wasn't looking for a murderer; he was looking for what killed the murderer.

The camera made a loud clicking noise, followed by a flash. William felt uncomfortable. Since the pandemic, he had to wear an extra screen in front of his face, and he was covered from top to bottom in a white quarantine suit. This made his job harder.

William observed an irregular wound on Daisy's leg, which had healed. He estimated it was about two weeks old.

Maybe she fell down, he thought, studying the bruising pattern.

He noticed something Fredrick had missed and put the

camera aside. Picking up the forceps, he collected the dirt underneath her toenails. Next, he cut her toenails and bagged them.

For the next hour, William prepared the slides for a skin biopsy. Fredrick had already sent her blood for a preliminary test for toxins, drugs, and alcohol to the local lab. Since William didn't know what he was looking for, he needed a wide spectrum of tests and collected more samples to send them to the City Morgue.

It had turned dark outside, but William hadn't noticed. Fredrick remained with him. William carefully placed the skin sample on the slide and added the stain. He turned towards the young coroner.

"How are we going?" Fredrick asked.

"We are doing well. What about the X-rays?"

"We have to wait for the technician on-call."

"Okay." William replied.

He turned and placed the slide under the microscope and adjusted the lens. It was just his first day at the morgue, and William was regretting it. Everything was very slow. He peered into the microscope while Fredrick came to stand close to him.

When William remained silent, Fredrick asked, "Anything?"

William sat straight. "Hm... the skin is lacerated, and the inner and outer cells are destroyed as if..."

"She had a severe allergic reaction," Fredrick said, completing the sentence.

William nodded.

The door opened, and Norris stepped in. "Don't you boys want to go home and sleep?" he asked.

William looked at the time it was past midnight.

6th February 2020

After putting Daisy's body back in the freezer and saying goodnight to Fredrick, William headed home with Norris. They remained silent until William spoke.

"What did Mr. Murphy say?"

Norris shook his head in dismay and updated him. "Did you find anything new?" Norris asked.

"Nothing yet. We are waiting for the X-rays."

Suddenly Norris pushed the car brakes and turned his head.

"What?" William asked, looking behind. The road was barren, dark, and fog whizzed along with the wind.

"Stay in the car," Norris instructed, and stepped out.

William sensed something was wrong and wasn't comfortable alone in the car. He opened the door and stepped into the cold, damp night. Tall trees towered on both sides of the road, and there were hardly any street-lights. Except for Norris, everyone else was a stranger, and this made him uneasy. For the first time, William grasped the stillness of the vicinity and swallowed hard. He was all alone out here, no help, no backup. He followed Norris, who had his hand on the gun.

"What is it?" William whispered.

"I think I saw someone."

William narrowed his eyes and tried to look into the gloomy forest.

"Are you sure?" he asked.

They heard a rustle, and Norris drew his gun. "Maybe someone went out for a walk," William muttered.

Norris stared at him. "At 1:30 am?"

The forest turned silent, and they waited. The rustling noise never returned, and William's pounding heart slowed down. After a while, they gave up and returned to the car.

15

EVIL NEVER SLEEPS

15th February 2020 (Present day)
Highway

Wiping the sweat off his forehead, the sheriff tried to stay focused, but his mind kept racing. He was terrified. He never knew such fear until today. Sweat trickled down his neck as he gripped the steering.

Focus, focus, he thought.

He had to keep going. He had to do this. William's plan depended on him. His eyes widened; his heart leaped to his throat.

"Oh no," he muttered.

The truck slowed down and came to a complete stop.

"Oh my god," cried Kyle.

A tilted car blocked more than half of the road. The driver was trying to get out of the broken window. She screamed in pain as she tried to free herself from the seatbelt. Norris's heart stopped in his chest. He recognized her; it was Mrs. Terresa Flores. An old friend, and the person who ran the Sheriff's office.

"Oh, no no no… this is not good," Kyle murmured.

Two figures emerged from the forest. Norris swallowed hard.

"This is not good," said Kyle.

The men approached Mrs. Flores. They walked awkwardly, hunched forward. One of them raised an ax.

"No!" Norris yelled, and jumped out of the car.

"Chief, no!" warned Kyle.

Norris pulled out the gun and shot the man in the leg. The man didn't scream, just wobbled and fell on the damp grass. Before Norris could deal with the second attacker, Kyle rushed ahead and knocked off the man.

"Terresa! Terresa! Are you okay?" Norris said, giving her a hand. She grabbed it and bit him. He yelled in pain.

She laughed like a crazy woman.

"You die! You die with us!" she bawled and grabbed his neck, sinking her nails into his skin.

"Flores… stop!" he cried out, pushing her away and pointed his gun at her white, pale face. Blood oozed out of her mouth. Her eyes were red, full of evil.

She smiled wickedly. "Do it… do it!"

Nightridge

The laptop beeped, and William gave a sign of relief. The update was complete, and Jack should be able to help them. He looked at the phone. No word from the sheriff.

He needs time, he thought.

William didn't know what evil he was facing. The

world had gone mad. He got on his knees, moved toward the laptop and accepted the video call from Jack.

"We are ready?" asked William

Jack Calvin sulked. William knew something was off. Jack's face appeared smaller and paler compared to the week before. The software engineer looked worried.

"Sorry William. You have to get to the server at the mayor's house," Jack said.

William gulped. "Why?"

"We cannot do this without the server."

William wished it were a simple task. He yearned for a reset button he could push and put his world back together. Unfortunately, there wasn't.

"How far is the house?" asked Tom, coming to his side.

"Around six blocks," William replied.

Tom frowned as his eyes moved toward the window.

"Jack, we will let you know when we get there."

Jack's face vanished, and the screen became dark.

Leaving the laptop on the floor, William got on the table and cautiously peered outside. A dead dog laid on the lawn. The windows of the houses across the street were broken. A cat meowed somewhere, clearly in distress. Screams were heard at a distance, and the fire was still raging. It appeared the mob had left the area for the time being.

A loud thud reverberated in the room. William stood against the wall. Hopefully, they hadn't seen him. A loud shriek resonated. He shivered and almost jumped when a heavy thump echoed.

Tom slowly stood up, ready with his gun. Fredrick

pushed himself against the table, as if wanting to disappear into it. William slowly peeped out the window, catching a glimpse of a figure staring at the dead dog. It was a man in torn clothes, holding a knife soaked with blood. The fog blew along with the soft breeze, and for a second, the man disappeared from William's view. The figure leaned over and sliced the dog into half in one stroke. William looked away. He focused on Tom, who was looking at his phone. His thoughts were drawn back towards the man. It was just one man. Where were the rest of them? Maybe they moved on. A part of him was pleased, but he sensed something was off. He stepped down from the table and grabbed the laptop.

Jack reappeared on the screen.

"Where are they?" William asked fearfully.

Jack's face blanched. "You don't want to know."

16

CONCERNED CITIZENS

6th February 2020
Meadow Cottage

Norris woke up and wrapped himself in the blanket. It was so nice and cozy; he didn't feel like getting out of bed. Then he thought of Nicholas.

Someone should check on him, he thought.

Loud roars of engines echoed outside. Norris sulked. He tore the sheets away and stood looking outside his bedroom window. Billy and his gang were riding again. The bikers rode with faces painted white, their long hair smeared red, and tattoos covering their bare arms and neck. On the sides of their bikes hung axes.

Norris had tried to take them away, but they declared they used it for cutting trees. Norris didn't believe them for a second. He had been expecting them to create chaos, get into fights. But they had been mostly peaceful.

He secretly wondered what they were trying to prove. Perhaps they wanted to show that they were daring, or possibly they wanted people to fear them. The truth was, they made the villagers nervous.

Each of them was an offender. A criminal. Known for their violence and uncontrolled anger. The villagers despised them, and many had complained. But Norris's hands were tied. Billy owned land on which the house and the garage were located. Norris needed a very good reason to throw them out of the village. For the last six months, except for being noisy and using foul language, the group had done nothing wrong. The bikes roared down the road, and soon there was silence again.

After getting ready for his day, he came downstairs. William was awake as well, which didn't surprise Norris. They cooked breakfast, and Norris was overjoyed to have company and eat food that actually tasted better.

"So, how is your family?" William asked.

Norris smiled. "Good. Safe."

He said no more. He wasn't in the mood to confide in anyone right now.

"Good to know."

"How are your friends?"

"They are good."

Norris waited, but when William remained quiet, he asked, "Where are they?"

William's face fell. "Far away."

"Where?"

"Roumoult is in Canada, Jack, and Alice in California, and Angelus in Mexico."

Norris smiled. Everyone was missing people they love. "Hey, you have a girlfriend. At least you are not alone."

"Yeah," William replied, not saying another word.

Norris sensed his discomfort and decided not to pursue the matter further.

Sheriff's Office

After dropping William at the morgue, Norris entered his office. Deputy Hector Mathews still looked pale.

Mrs. Terresa Flores, the administrator, greeted him. She was a middle-aged, old-fashioned woman with curly hair and a round face. He considered her like his own sister. She wished him a lovely morning with her usual grin. According to him, she was the liveliest person in the village and he adored her.

The other five members of the sheriff's department included Deputies Hector Mathews, Kyle Torres, Ron Mater, Nelson Force and Jeremy Luke.

"I don't know why we are worried? A girl just went crazy... she was probably on drugs," concluded Nelson Force.

Norris smiled patiently. "Hector and Kyle, did you get a list of witnesses?"

"Yes, they will be here in the afternoon," answered Hector.

"Good. Good. What else have you found out?" Norris looked at Ron Mater.

"I have put in a warrant to get access to her phone records. It's still processing."

Norris nodded as he walked through the small hall. He opened the door and stepped into his messy, yet cozy, little office. Rubbing his hands, he turned on the heater. Mrs. Flores followed him in and closed the door.

"Mayor Rogers called."

"Oh, did he? How very interesting..." Norris replied, still sleepy and thinking about his next cup of coffee.

"Henry called and asked you to send the city doctor back."

"Sure. He can do that when he becomes the sheriff. As long as I am the sheriff, we do what I say."

She rolled her eyes and handed him today's messages. He flipped through them one by one.

"Some *concerned* citizens," she mocked.

He read through the complaint list. They were about insignificant matters. Mrs. Claw thought other people were stealing her chickens. Mr. Inking thought the police were being unreasonable about the lockdown and things should go back to normal. Mrs. Lawrence was grumbling about several missed calls and thought that someone was watching her. She was sure someone entered her garden last night. Norris shook his head, but the last one caught his attention. Mr. Oberon thought he saw someone walking in the forest last night.

Mrs. Flores spoke, "One more thing, Ms. Pritchard asked if she could organize the children's art evening at the local school."

Norris frowned.

"Principal Larry Jackson has already agreed, and she just thought she should let you know. She said they will follow all the rules of social distancing and sanitize their hands frequently. They will wear masks, and if anyone is sick or shows symptoms, all of them will get tested and quarantined."

Norris pondered.

"I think an evening out for the kids would be good for everyone. We should be a bit more lenient."

"Fine… fine… just tell her to make sure it doesn't get too crowded."

"Thank you, Chief. I'll be at my desk if you need me," she said and left him alone.

Norris picked up the phone and called Mr. Oberon. "Hey Ray?"

"How are you doing, Sheriff?"

"I am well. Thanks. You?"

"Good. Good."

"I got your message. You thought you saw someone in the forest?"

"Yeah. Let me explain. You know I have a small bladder. Last night, I had to wake up to take a leak. So, I am doing my business, and I see something move in the woods."

Norris turned around, stood up, and looked at the map. Ray's house was two miles away from where he believed he had seen someone in the forest. "What time was this?"

"Around 3 am…"

Norris pursed his lips. "What did you see?"

"A man walking in the forest. But there was something

odd about him."

"What?"

"The way he walked. It was weird."

"What do you mean?"

"As if he were hypnotized or something. As if he was sleepwalking, unaware of the world around him."

Norris was stumped. He thanked Ray for calling and hung up. For several minutes, he sat back in his seat wondering. No one he knew sleep walked in the village, then who was this stranger?

County Morgue

William adjusted his gloves and wore protective gear over his face, and eyes before he approached the body. He was finally ready to do the autopsy. Usually the process was faster, but since they had to wait for the on-call radiologist, the autopsy was delayed. Finally, the technician showed up this morning, and they could start the autopsy.

After an hour, William held the girl's heart in his hand. The power of this small and light organ always amazed him. He weighed it and wrote notes down about its physical appearance. Next, he reached for the liver and carefully weighed it. Putting it on a tray, he took a section of the liver and prepared the tissue for examination. As he progressed, he took tissue samples from all the organs.

His phone vibrated on the stand. He reached out for a tissue, covered his fingers, and pushed the green button.

The video call was connected, and a friendly face appeared on the phone.

"Hey... how are you?" Roumoult Cranston said, smiling.

William was used to getting calls from him often during the day, and it was good. When the first wave of the pandemic hit, Roumoult, and his father were in Canada. Roumoult was one of its first victims, and he developed a sudden fever. He was taken to the hospital and held in quarantine after he had tested positive for the virus.

William recalled almost having a nervous breakdown. He wanted to rush to Canada, but the borders were closed. William wasn't certain if his best friend would survive. During that time, he was on the phone constantly, talking with the doctors and Roumoult's father. William would never forget that week. It was a nightmare. His only comfort was that Roumoult had his family with him. His friend remained in the hospital during his recovery and then quarantined. William was sure he had lost weight, and his skin looked paler.

"I am good," William said.

His friend's eyes surveyed the room. "Where are you?"

"Nightridge."

Roumoult sat back.

William noticed a different wallpaper behind Roumoult. As far as he knew, after recovering and being discharged from the hospital, they were staying in a hotel. "Where are you?"

Roumoult rolled his eyes.

"Well?"

"The borders are still closed, and we couldn't stay at the hotel anymore. So, we moved."

"Where?'

"Oh, you are going to love this. I am at a farmhouse thirty miles away from Quebec or any kind of civilization!"

Oh, my god. Canada was in trouble, thought William.

Roumoult was of the same age as him, with striking features and deep green eyes. He was raised in a mansion and his parents showered him with everything money could buy, and their love for him knew no bounds. Roumoult had never seen hardship, not the way William had. And now he was in a farmhouse. God help the animals.

"Don't give me that look."

The screen fluttered.

"Well, desperate times call for desperate measures. Stay away from the horses," William replied, picking up the pancreas to weigh it.

"It's not the horses you should be worried about."

William straightened. He heard screams, yells, and cries in the background. Suddenly four children surrounded Roumoult. He shut his eyes, and William noticed his face reddened.

Oh my god, William thought.

The children waved toward him; William waved back. Then they were gone in a flash. Roumoult took a sharp breath in and held his head.

"How is it?"

Roumoult looked toward the ceiling. "I am sharing a room with a six-year-old. The bed creaks, and the house has a centuries-old central heating system. The floor is always cold. All the doors need new hinges. They cook on a stove that I have never seen in my life. The food sucks, and Mrs. Wilson needs a new coffee machine."

William had to control himself from laughing. The screen fluttered again. For a moment he lost his friend.

Roumoult moped. "I don't want to sound ungrateful. Mrs. Wilson is dad's friend and an amiable lady, but I never thought I would say this, I miss the hospital!"

William chuckled.

"It was clean and free of little humans!"

William laughed so hard he had to put the organ back in the body to make sure he didn't drop it.

"Oh yeah, you can laugh."

He stopped and regained his composure. At least talking with Roumoult gave him something else to think about.

"What brought you to Nightridge?"

"A dead body."

Roumoult stared at him. "There are enough of them in New York."

"This one is different."

"Is it human?"

William chuckled. "Yes."

"Another COVID death?"

"No. No. It's murder..." William paused. A bell rang in his head. Roumoult was just recovering, and it was best not to arouse his curiosity. A melting body with burned eyes and a crazy killer. A puzzle waiting to be solved. That was Roumoult's cup of tea. "It's a murder investigation, and Sheriff Cunningham needed my help."

"Well… well… the criminal world hasn't turned dull after all. What have you got?"

"Hm, it's a straightforward case, nothing for you to worry about."

"If it wasn't complicated, why did Sheriff Cunningham call you?"

"He needed a forensic pathologist."

Roumoult smirked. "You wanted to get out of the city."

"Yes. I really needed to leave. It's crazy."

"And you left your girlfriend in the middle of a pandemic?"

William rolled his eyes. "She doesn't need me." He replied, checking his notes.

Roumoult changed the subject. "Did you have to skin her?"

"That is how she was found."

"Really? That's interesting? Have you found anything yet?"

William gulped. "No."

"I see. What are you looking for?"

"I'm not sure. I'll have to do a wide spectrum of tests." William paused and then said, "Have you been in touch with Jack?"

"Ah… yeah. He and Alice are still in California at the NEO Tech. We are hoping to finish a project."

"What was it about?"

"Improving drones."

William faced the camera. "They have been around for a while."

"Yeah. But they have their limits. A drone is an

unmanned aircraft or a flying robot that can be remotely controlled up to thirty miles. Our drones are smaller, lighter, faster, have an inbuilt sensor, GPS and a camera. They can be programmed to work as a group or individually and have a small loading bay which can be used to release pesticides or airborne vectors."

"Sounds very cool," William stated.

Roumoult frowned.

"What happened?" William inquired.

"We can't test! The drones arrived before this stupid pandemic hit! Unless Jack or I test the program and the drones, I cannot sign off the project. We are stuck and our clients have started complaining. But there is nothing we can do."

"Where are the drones now?"

"They are at Cranston enterprises."

"Well, what is Jack doing in California?"

"He is working on the next idea."

"What idea?"

Roumoult smiled. "He didn't tell me. I think he is trying to keep himself occupied."

"What about Alice? Is she happy there?"

"She grumbles and gets over it."

"Have you heard from Angelus?"

"No, not since he got the gig in Mexico. I am guessing he's stuck there."

"He is a Private Investigator and he said a friend needed his help in a matter."

"Yeah. I think it's good. New York is not safe."

"Nowhere is safe."

"So, tell me about this case."

"Fine. Daughter kills the mom, attacks the father, and then dies."

"That is curious. Where is her skin?" Roumoult asked again.

William shut his eyes. "I can't explain…it's shredded."

"Shredded? Like a snake?"

"Yeah. But the snake gets a new one."

Fredrick stepped in with the X-rays, handed them over to William. He noticed William was talking to someone and left. William appreciated the privacy. He placed one of the X-ray films on the display box.

"What is your next step?"

"Roumoult, you need to rest."

"Not you too. Please. Give me something to do. Anything. The courts have shut down and all my cases are on hold. Everything sucks, and it's boring!"

"Roumoult, if I find something that calls in for your expertise, I will certainly let you know. Until then, how about focusing on some other project? I am sure you can access the Cranston Enterprise's server remotely."

Roumoult's face turned to stone. "The internet speed over here is 1.85 Mbps."

Roumoult's call may not have helped him professionally, but it lifted William's spirits.

William focused on the X-rays. The bones of the feet looked normal, with no apparent fractures or bone bruising. He turned to his file and made a note. He spent the next few minutes looking at the tibia, fibula, and femur. The bones of both legs appeared healthy. He didn't note any injuries to the knee joints. Frowning, he pulled off the films and looked at the hips. Shaking his head, he put up the chest X-ray. It was normal, and he began wondering if the films were going to help him. The last two X-rays showed the cervical spine and the head. His jaw dropped, and he peered into the X-ray.

"What the hell is that?" he muttered.

17

WHO CAN WE SAVE?

15th February 2020 (Present day)
Highway

Standing near the tilted car on the highway, Norris forced himself not to pull the trigger. Before Mrs. Flores could attack him, he flipped the gun and knocked her off. Puffing, Norris looked at the unconscious woman. It was unbelievable. At first, he thought he should just leave her here. But was it safe? Maybe he should tie her to a tree. What if someone else killed her? He wondered what he should do.

The man who lay unconscious on the side of the road was familiar to him. Larka was one of Billy's men. He had seen him several times in the village. Norris grabbed the ax and signaled Kyle.

They left the men behind and carried Mrs. Flores to the truck. They carefully put her on the back seat. He glimpsed at the time; he had very little. Norris jumped behind the wheel. The young deputy sat in the passenger seat. Glancing at the unconscious lady, Norris turned the key and drove around the tilted car. He glanced at the smoke in his rare mirror.

"Just two more miles. I hope we have no more surprises," said Kyle, wiping the sweat of his forehead.

Darkness surrounded the truck, and the fog was becoming thicker. Norris peeked into the rear-view mirror. No one was following them. Peering over his shoulder, he saw Mrs. Flores was still unconscious. He wished she remained that way.

What was happening to them? If William's plan works, can they get back to normal? What if he fails? Perhaps he can't save them? What if this spreads throughout the world and another pandemic ensues?

He shook his head and tried to calm his racing heart. Norris thought about his family and he had to stay alive for them. He had to get through this. He floored the accelerator, and the truck charged ahead, cutting through the thick haze.

Nightridge

The door of the autopsy room opened with a cracking noise. Armed, William peeped out. The fresh smell of blood mixed with garbage filled the air. The corridor was silent. He glanced at the group behind him. Fredrick carried the laptop while Tom was ready with his gun.

This is a bad idea, William thought.

But he had no choice. He tiptoed toward the door and he opened it slightly and peeped into the dark night. For now, it was quiet. Jack had already told him the mob had left the area, which gave him some comfort. They stepped out and walked along the wall. They stopped at the corner of the building and observed the terrain ahead.

The smoke and ash bothered William's nostrils. Garbage littered the road, and houses were on fire. He looked up and down the street. His eyes became fixed.

"No! No!" William cried, rushing towards a burning car. "Oh, my god! This is unbelievable. No!!"

"What happened?" Tom asked.

"They burned my car! They burned my car!" William complained.

Tom calmed down and said, "Oh, good. It's about time you got rid of that old bucket."

William scowled at him, "Tom!"

"Pipe down! We have bigger things to worry about. How do we get to the school?" Tom asked.

William was frustrated. He had that car since he graduated from medical school. It had been his friend for over a decade. His friends always complained about it. Jack said it was responsible for ten percent of the noise pollution in the city. Joan claimed it was a moving garbage bin and Roumoult complained it was the reason ice in Antarctica was melting. He didn't care, he loved his Hyundai.

The three men rushed south, avoiding the main road. Most of the houses were abandoned. The doors were left open, and lights brightened the interiors, but they saw no one.

Sweat dripped down his neck, and William felt as if his

legs would give away. He wished they could use a car, but it would attract attention.

William slowed his pace when they came to the small shopping center and a pharmacy. The door to the pharmacy was broken and lights flickered indoors. Two figures lay on the ground, covered with blood. Without thinking, William rushed to them. Both of them had sustained head injuries. He checked their pulses; they were alive.

"William, we have to go." Fredrick said.

"But…"

"We can't help them," Fredrick cried out.

William followed them outside, and they walked past the shopping center. The door was ajar, and the interior was dark. They rushed down the road. The school was two houses down the street. Shouts from a distance made him flinch. William tried to ignore the chaos around them and increased his pace. Despite a racing heart and being out of breath, he didn't stop running. Tom and Fredrick were not that far behind.

In minutes, they neared the school building. When they heard voices, they reduced their pace. Breathless, William leaned against a tree and observed. The school was a square, two-story brick building. It was dark inside. Staying out of sight, he watched. It looked quiet, but he wasn't sure. They could be hiding. A loud crashing noise startled the trio. From the dark forest, they saw figures moving.

"We are out of time," muttered Tom.

"No. We must wait," William said.

They waited. The leaves swayed, and the figures soon disappeared into the shadows.

"Now," William muttered.

They darted across the street, and William grabbed the door. It was locked.

"Damn!" he muttered. He moved quickly and crawled through a broken window. The others followed.

He waited until the others were inside and closed the blinds. William noted they were in a classroom with two large windows. The benches were scattered in a zigzag fashion. Colorful pictures covered the walls. William froze when he saw shadows. He glued himself against the wall while the other two men dropped to the floor. The shadows lurked outside the window. He heard them breathe. Suddenly the shadows disappeared, and he heard footsteps moving away. He let out a long breath. Tom and Fredrick emerged from behind the benches.

"That was close," murmured Fredrick.

"Don't worry, we will get out of this," William said. He had to keep Fredrick calm, they needed him.

Fredrick gulped, "I hope you are right. I really hope."

"Fredrick, there is no going back,"

Their eyes met, "I know," he replied.

The men stood beside the window and peered outside into the darkness. It was silent. William bit his lips and wondered why a part of the crazy mob was hanging around the school. Did they know the children were here? He hoped they hadn't found them.

William crossed the classroom, slowly opened the door, and looked up and down the passageway. They were in luck.

"Where are the children?" Tom asked.

William gestured them to follow him. He walked down

the corridor and took a sharp left and then a right. At the end of the passageway was a staircase, and below it was an old wooden door. He gradually opened it and came down the gloomy stairs. It was full of a foul stench, dirt, and litter. Reaching for his phone, he turned on the light. He noticed a cluster of mops, buckets, and cleaning materials in a corner. The ground was uneven, and he had to step carefully over the broken tiles. He turned and saw another small door. Glancing behind, he twisted the knob.

"Ms. Pritchard," William said in a low voice as he entered.

He heard a low moan as Tom closed the door. They cautiously came down the small number of steps. William stopped when he heard hushed sobs.

"Ms. Pritchard?" William whispered.

A small light came to life. He saw the pale, frightened face of the teacher. Tom turned on the light on his phone. As the light grew in the dark room, tiny figures became visible. The children stood close to the teacher; terror filled in their little eyes.

18

A NIGHT IN THE FOREST

6th February 2020
Local Hospital

Daisy's head X-ray bothered him. What was it? It was embedded deep in her brain. The only way to get answers was to do a brain MRI. It was tedious, but he had to place all the organs back inside and stitch Daisy's body and get it ready for a short trip to the local hospital. The ambulance wobbled a bit, and he grabbed the handle. Daisy was strapped to the trolley. The air inside was turning foul, and he hoped they would get to the hospital soon.

The MRI center was on the first floor of the local hospital, and when he expressed his wish to conduct an MRI scan on a dead body, no one was delighted. The administrator of the hospital refused it. But then William spoke with Norris, and within ten minutes, he got the approval.

As soon as they got there, he helped the driver unload the body from the ambulance and carry it inside.

William sensed the nurses and doctors staring, but he ignored them. The hefty elevator moved upward and stopped on the first floor. The doors opened, they walked down a long passageway to the radiology department.

A very agitated technician greeted them. He threw around orders coldly and refused to touch the body. Fortunately, the task was simple for William, since he was wearing protective gear and he had handled corpses for the last decade.

Once the corpse was ready, William stood with the technician. The test began. The machine whirred and started taking pictures. Black and white images began appearing on the monitor, and the interior of Daisy's head emerged.

The machine stopped with a loud thud, and he felt his heart stop. The horror on the technician's face was unmissable. He gulped and slowly peered into the screen. He reached for the keyboard and flipped through the images. His mouth went dry as he tried to comprehend what he was looking at. The MRI showed three objects embedded in her brain.

Sheriff's Office

Norris needed more coffee. The interviews were draining his energy. Daisy had few friends, and all of them were in his book, naïve and ignorant teenagers. Tracey Duke was one of those friends. She sat in front of him, wearing a white t-shirt and jeans, and looked like she was bored. To protect against the spread of the virus, a glass screen stood between him and the girl. Two mics stood on the desk. Both of them were wearing masks, and he had made sure she had sanitized.

"She was her normal self," said Tracy, looking around. "Are you recording this?"

"No."

"Oh. I thought I was going to be on TV…"

"No. This is a murder investigation."

"What's the big deal? Daisy turned nuts and shot her mother."

"Were you two close?" asked Norris.

"Yeah. Yeah. We were besties."

"Besties?" Norris never understood why young people used slang. Perhaps it made them feel cool, or it was all about appearances.

"Okay. Did you guys see each other before her death?"

"Nope."

"Are you sure?"

"Yeah. Because of the lockdown."

"Don't lie."

"I am not lying."

"Okay. When was the last time you spoke to her?"

Tracey looked uncomfortable. "Last week."

"Did she tell you if she had left the house?"

Tracey avoided eye contact. "Yeah. She told me she hung out with Luke the other day."

"Where did she go?" He asked.

"Into the woods."

"The woods are vast. Where exactly did she go?"

"She said they drove around… or about an hour."

"They took the car, and no one noticed?"

"I don't know! That's what she told me!"

"When was this?"

"A week ago."

"Okay. Did she say anything else?"

"Na. The usual stuff. How boring it is. How much we hate the lockdown. Homeschooling sucks and we hated doing assignments. There are just too many of them. We also discussed movies and the series we watched and made some silly jokes. That was it."

"Try harder."

Tracey sulked. "What do you want me to say?"

"Did she sound stressed, sad, or disturbed in any way?"

"No."

"Did she tell you the about her trip?"

Tracey became thoughtful. "I think they went near the waterfall, made out for a while, and drove back."

"During the day or night…"

"Night."

"Night?"

"Yeah."

"Anything else you would like to share?"

"No."

Luke was next on his list. Chewing gum, Luke sat in front of Norris, wearing a black jacket and jeans. His hair had too much gel, and his curious blue eyes glazed around. He was neither muscular nor tall and had no distinctive features. The young man appeared to be happy. It didn't matter that he was in a police station or his girlfriend was dead. As far as he knew, Luke had no girlfriends. Just flings. He was the high school "bad boy," and the girls were attracted to him like he was a magnet.

"You know why you are here, right?" Norris asked, expecting that question to bother him. But the demeanor of the young man didn't change.

"Yeah. I know. Daisy… is…"

Luke's face turned soft, surprising Norris.

"What do you think happened to her?"

"She turned into a lunatic."

Norris ignored his comment. "How long did you know Daisy?"

"Since we were children."

"Had she ever acted like this before?"

"No. Not really. I should say nice things about her… right?"

"You should tell the truth."

"Well, she was normal all her life until that morning."

"Did she misbehave during your night trips?"

Luke's face filled with surprise. "Oh. Oh… No, we did nothing like that. My parents forbid it."

Norris smiled. "Try again."

"No. We didn't."

"When did you last see her?"

"Before the lockdown."

"Try again."

Luke gulped. "Look. Sir. I was just so bored."

"So?"

"We went out a couple of times… just for fun. It was plain fun. Nothing else. Life is so fucking boring nowadays. I should have been on a camping trip with my friends. Instead, I am stuck with my parents all day and night. I had to get out!"

"Where did you go?"

"To the woods…"

"Where exactly…"

"Well, I sneaked my car out of the garage, and then we drove for about thirty minutes and stopped near the waterfalls."

"At night?"

"Yeah. It was fun to be outside. To be free. We're young. We want to live."

"What did you do?"

"We went for a swim."

"Swim?"

"Yes."

"Tell me, where did you go?" Norris asked, giving him a map. The boy pointed to the location.

"How many times?"

"Three times…"

"Daisy was with you every time?"

"Daisy? No. She came only once."

Norris's head started throbbing. Why couldn't teenagers keep their lives simple?

"Who else went there with you?"

"Lara and Vicky."

He knew both girls. In his perspective, Daisy was one of the good ones. "Okay. What else did you do?"

Luke smiled proudly. "We did stuff…."

"How long did you stay in the forest?"

"Um… we must have reached there about 11 pm and left around 5 am."

"Did she leave your side?"

"No. I don't think so."

"Are you sure?"

"Yeah. Yeah."

"Where did you sleep?"

"Well, it was a sort of camping trip. I had a sleeping bag and a tent."

"Okay. She might have slipped out."

"Daisy? No! She didn't have it in her."

"Really?"

"She was afraid of the dark."

"Did you leave her alone?"

"No, I didn't."

"Did Daisy behave differently after that night?"

"Na. We were cool."

"Did she say anything or do anything differently?"

"Na."

"Okay. When did you go to the forest?"

"A week before the murder."

"And you didn't see her since?"

"No."

"Did you call her?"

"No."

"Texted her?"

"No."

"Are you sure?"

"Yeah. Yeah."

"Interesting. We found text messages from you on her phone."

Luke gulped. "Oh yeah. Yeah… we just talked."

"No. You fought," Norris corrected him.

Luke rolled his eyes. "Look. Girls get too touchy. You spend some time with them, and they feel you owe them something. Okay. I didn't know she was that type. I just wanted to have fun. She got all emotional when she found out we were not exclusive."

"Of course."

"It was nothing... she wasn't even good at it."

Norris felt a bit annoyed. "Did you call her back after that?"

"Hey. If you have her phone. You already know I didn't."

"She might have used the landline."

"She didn't call..."

"But you messaged her... and kept messaging her."

Luke hung his head. "Look. We go to the same school and hang out with the same people... I just didn't want things to end like that. She... she didn't understand it was just sex."

"Not for her. She was fifteen."

"Hey, she was almost sixteen."

"You shouldn't have played with her feelings."

"Okay. I am sorry. I might have upset her a bit."

But not enough to shoot her mom, Norris thought.

"I didn't mean it."

"Anything useful you can tell me?"

"That's all I have got."

"Did she speak to you about her mother?"

"Nope."

"About her father?"

"Nope."

Norris balled his hands in a fist and said "I see."

. . .

Disappointed, Norris spoke with Daisy's teacher. Mrs. York told him Daisy was a quiet, good and studious kid. She seemed a bit distracted in the last few weeks, but besides that, she was doing well. During the lockdown, Mrs. York had difficulty with many students, but Daisy seemed to have no trouble with her studies. Her mother never complained about her, nor did Daisy ever miss a class. She submitted all her assignments on time and got along with everyone. Lately, she seemed sad and distracted. Norris thought it could be because of her feelings for Luke.

Daisy's third friend was the first person to shed some light on the truth. Ms. Patrice Xavier was in tears. The young girl had known Daisy all her life. Patrice's sadness seemed to fill the room. Her mother sat beside her, with her hands clamped together.

"Patrice, how are you today?" Norris asked.

"Fine."

"I am sorry, but I have to ask you some questions. Is that okay?"

She nodded gradually.

"What can you tell me about Daisy?"

She raised her eyebrows. "Daisy was always so kind, friendly, and gentle. In the last few days of her life, she changed. She was quiet, sad, and angry."

"She had a fight with Luke," Norris said.

"Oh. I don't think so. This was after that. She had her cry about it on the phone, and I told her she should have expected it."

"Did she tell you about her night?"

Patrice rolled her eyes. "Yes. Unfortunately, everything. How lovely it was? How it felt? Everything. For her, it was love at first sight."

"Anything else?"

"She mentioned she kept hearing noises."

Norris leaned forward. "What noises?"

"Some kind of humming…"

"Could it have been an animal?"

"She didn't know."

"Did she follow it?"

"No. Daisy hates the dark. She only went with Luke because she liked him."

"Luke said they went for a swim."

"He did. She didn't."

Norris didn't know who to believe. "So, you think she didn't get in the water."

"She always said that she hated to swim in the dark and cold."

"What about her relationship with her mom?"

Patrice raised her eyebrows. "Well, Mrs. Murphy was a bit, you know… like any other mother… always lecturing."

Norris could relate. As a parent, he often finds telling his daughter what was best for her. "How did Daisy take it?"

Patrice hung her head. "Not good really. She felt…"

"Yes?"

"She felt she could do nothing right to make her mother happy."

"What do you mean?"

"You know how she was? Her mother?"

"According to everyone, Mrs. Murphy was a lovely, gentle soul, and did a lot of good things for this society,"

Patrice nodded. "That's all true, but she expected too much from Daisy. She often felt that her mom wanted her to be like her. Daisy… just wanted to have fun."

"You think her mother pushed her too much?"

"Yeah… since… since… she became a woman."

"Did their relationship change then, over time?"

"Yeah. Especially during the lockdown. Daisy said that her mother scrutinized everything she did and hounded her with questions. It was too much. They had constant fights. She hated her mom."

"She told this to you?"

"Yeah."

"But Tracey said Daisy had no issues."

Patrice frowned. "Yeah… Tracey is like a frenemy."

Norris was confused. "What is that?"

"It's a person you cannot trust. The minute they get a chance, they turn on you and stab you in the back."

"I see. So, you are saying Daisy would never confide in Tracey."

"Nope."

"What about boys? Was she seeing anyone except Luke?"

"Daisy wasn't like that."

"Okay. What about her father?"

"Oh, she loved her father. Mr. Murphy was very supportive of her. He loved her to bits, and he was so understanding. She said if it weren't for her dad, she would have run away."

Norris raised his eyebrows. Daisy loved him more than anything, and yet she had attacked him and tried to kill him. Why?

"Did she have any issues in school?"

"Ah... yeah, she hated the physical activity teacher, Mr. Reich."

"Why?"

"She felt he was unfair to her."

"How?"

"No matter how much effort she made during the class, he never gave her good grades."

"It made her feel bad?"

"Yes. Some teachers like doing that."

19

SAVING OUR FUTURE

15th February 2020 (Present day)
Highway

Norris's truck cut through a thick haze, and the shadows no longer followed them. Norris reduced speed, swung the steering, and entered the forest. The truck drove over the muddy terrain.

The sky was clear. Darkness surrounded the truck, and the smog was becoming heavier. Despite the cold, Norris was perspiring. He glanced into the rare mirror. He was not being trailed. So far, it was working, and it should be okay. All he could do was hope.

The phone buzzed. He glanced at it and saw a message from William: *Delayed. Had to get to the children to safety.*

"Fuck!" he muttered.

"What happened?" Kyle asked.

"William went to get the children."

"Oh, no. How did they find them?"

"I don't know... William can handle it," Norris said, lying to himself again.

"Can he?"

Norris stayed quiet and kept driving. He had to slow down; the fog was thick, and he couldn't see the path. The bushes and the muddy terrain made driving an arduous task.

"We should be careful," said Kyle, looking around them. He clutched the gun tightly.

"Don't worry. We are alone."

Norris swung the steering, and the truck turned left. The bridge wasn't far away.

On the rough road, the truck jolted and shook. Norris grabbed the steering hard, trying to maintain speed. The rocky terrain forced him to go even slower. Then the terrain descended. The truck shuddered, and it struggled to move over the muddy ground.

Several minutes passed, and Norris hit the brakes. The tires skidded slightly, and the truck came to a stop near the river bank. Puffing, both men glared at the water rushing down the creek. They were finally here.

Nightridge

In the hidden basement of the school, William's concern grew. He quickly grabbed Tom's phone and turned off the light. Tom was about to protest when he pointed to a narrow window near the roof.

"Shush..." he told the small group.

Tiny sobs filled the dark room. William moved toward Ms. Pritchard, and the children grabbed him. His heart melted. They were away from their parents, alienated, terrified, and needed normal adults. They were all these little children had.

William was trying to manage the situation, but he believed he was failing. He didn't have kids, and he knew nothing about parenting.

"We can't stay here," Ms. Pritchard said, whispering, "they are circling like vultures."

"Do they know you are here?"

"We didn't make a sound, I promise."

William wondered if they were scouting buildings. They did the same at the morgue and then moved to the houses. Now, they were at the school. They heard a pounding, and the group snuggled together.

"They may know we are here," whispered Ms. Pritchard.

"Shush... did you tell anyone about the art class at the school?"

"The entire village knew, especially the parents. They dropped them here before they..." She paused.

They heard a door close. William pushed the teacher and children behind him. Fredrick stood in the corner guarding the computer with his life, Tom stood in front, ready with his weapon. The footsteps came to a stop; they heard a muffled click. Tom glanced at him, and William gulped. No matter what happened to them, he couldn't let them hurt the children.

20

ANOMALIES

6th February 2020
County Hospital

Norris watched Nicholas for a few minutes through the side window. The TV was on, and Nicholas was staring out of the window. Norris followed his gaze and noticed the clear blue sky and the greenery. It was a pleasant sight. A shadow fell over Norris, and he turned to face the mayor.

Wow, he is really interested in this case. I wonder why?

"Hello," Norris said.

"Sheriff, you called in a Medical Examiner from the city?"

Norris knew this was coming. "We have an unusual death. I thought it was best to get an expert opinion."

"You could have sent him skin and tissue samples,

pictures of the body or the body itself. Why did you bring him here?"

Norris tried not to lose his composure. "Henry, there is something awfully wrong with that body. We need to find out what happened to Daisy and make sure it's not contagious."

Henry looked unimpressed. "Well... I don't think it's necessary. You are wasting our time and our resources. You should focus more on the pandemic, the lockdown. It needs your attention. Forget about the case!"

Norris folded his arms and gaped at him.

"Sheriff, I think you should drop this."

"I can't."

"Well... fine... have it your way. If this all goes to hell, it's going to be your fault!" Henry yelled, and walked away.

Norris stood, wondering. Henry's behavior was strange, but it wasn't new.

"Parents shouldn't have to bury their children," he thought.

Tears welled up in his eyes, and he controlled himself. He had to face another man who had suffered a similar tragedy.

Norris pushed himself and entered the room.

"How are you today?" he asked.

Nicholas sighed. "I am okay."

He dragged a chair and sat beside the bed.

"You never see this coming. You never think it would happen to you. But when it happens, you think of all the ways you could have stopped it. If I had woken up early, Mary would still be alive."

"True. Forgive me, I have to ask. Were Daisy and her mother fighting?"

Nicholas looked at him. "No. Not really. There was some bickering."

"A witness says that Mrs. Murphy was pressuring Daisy."

"Ah… oh… I see. I know. I know what they say. She expected too much from her daughter. And why shouldn't she?"

Norris sat, thinking it was better not to comment.

"Daisy was the best daughter a father could hope for. Mary wanted to make sure she stayed on track. She felt someone could easily manipulate Daisy, and she wanted to make her strong. Independent."

"Did Mary push her too hard?"

"No. I don't think so."

Norris nodded.

"Whoever told you that my darling was bothering Daisy is lying! She never harmed our child… she was just protecting her. Mary was always protecting her."

"Okay. Tell me, was Daisy terrified of the dark?"

Nicholas's face showed surprise. "Terrified? No. Not at all."

"She wasn't afraid of the dark?"

"No. Since she was a little girl , we used to go on hunting trips in the woods. We would come back late, and she was never scared."

"What about swimming?"

"Daisy loved swimming."

"Really?"

"Yes. She would jump into the water every chance she

got!"

"She would swim anywhere?"

"Wherever it was safe."

"I see. Do you have any pictures of her swimming?"

"Heaps…" he replied, pointing toward the phone on the table.

After Nicholas unlocked the phone, Norris flipped through dozens of pictures of Daisy enjoying swimming in the water. He paused when he saw dozens of photos of her in the waterfall in the forest.

County Morgue

William had to bring Daisy's body back to the morgue quickly and begin as soon as possible. It had been over three days since her death. Her organs would have started disintegrating. He had to act fast.

He quickly got back into protective gear. The morgue was cold, and he began parting her hair. He turned her head and picked up the scalpel, making an incision under her left lobe. In seconds, he skillfully made a cut from ear to ear. He slowly separated the anterior scalp, cutting through the tissue. Soon he was done, then worked toward opening the posterior scalp.

Soon the entire skull was exposed. He carefully marked the lines above the ears for cutting the skull. Then he used the scalpel to deepen the cuts.

Every time he did this step, William was hesitant. Gulping, he selected the oscillating saw. Carefully, he cut through the skull. If he made the cut too deep, he could damage the dura mater and eventually the brain. That might affect the results.

Once he was satisfied, he put the saw aside and picked up the surgical hammer and a chisel. He placed the hammer on the cuts and struck it on the chisel. He flipped the chisel and used the other side to separate the dura mater from the skull. Finally, he pulled the skull cap away to expose the brain.

He observed the hematoma in her left hemisphere. The rest of the brain appeared to be unaffected. He then began cutting the nerves and tissues to separate the brain from the skull.

Soon Daisy's brain was in his hand. After measuring its weight and completing the primary examinations, he set it on a sterile tray. Acting quickly, he reached for the huge jar full of formalin and carefully placed the brain in it. The formalin would keep the brain tissue intact. Since William didn't know what he was dealing with and how many samples he would need, he thought it was best to fix the brain before he used it for further examination. The formalin would bind the proteins in the organ and help preserve it for a longer period. After tightly closing the jar, he placed it in the refrigerator. He closed the door and stood nervously. The next forty-eight hours would be testing.

He would have to keep an eye on the sample, making sure it wasn't stolen or destroyed. Only he and the MRI technician knew about the anomalies, but he had to be careful. He stepped forward and turned the key to lock the refrigerator.

He secretly wondered if he could do anything else.

Then something occurred to him. He didn't want to rush to the hospital in case he needed more scans. William wrote an email to Johnathan, his assistant in the city, to order a hand-held optical scanner. It worked more or less like a sonogram but was more powerful, mobile, and lighter. It could be handy in situations like this. Once he was done, William got up, stretched, and left.

Nightridge, Town Center

William and Norris took a walk around the village. The population was just over five thousand. Around the morgue and the sheriff's department were only a dozen houses. The rest of the houses were scattered across the land, separated from each other by clusters of trees. The town hall was in the center of the town. It was a building with a large antique clock. About one mile away was a tall network tower. From here, it appeared to touch the clouds.

The gravel under their feet cracked as they strolled. They discussed the case for a while, but then fell silent. The air was chilly, clean, and the wind carried nothing but silence.

William was glad he came out here. The equipment here was ancient. It made his life miserable and slow, but yet there was something he liked. Perhaps it was the simplicity or maybe he enjoyed being alone.

Two bikes approached them, and he noticed Norris's face turn stern. William noticed the two men who walked toward him. They wore sleeveless t-shirts and jeans with chains hanging from the belts. Their bikes looked heavy, and axes hung on them. William swallowed hard.

A man, maybe a little older than him, with brown eyes, long hair, and a box-shaped stood before William. He glared at him as if he was going to eat him alive. William smelled alcohol on his breath.

"Who are you?" he asked.

"Billy," intervened Norris, "What are you doing out here? You should be indoors."

Billy didn't take his eyes off William. He glanced at the man beside him. He was shorter, bulkier, with rough brown hair.

"Why did you bring in this scum from the city?" Billy stated.

William's heartbeat quickened.

"Billy, mind your own business."

He turned to Norris. "Sheriff, I will not. This is our territory."

"No. This village belongs to the people of Nightridge. It is no one's territory!"

Billy turned to William, who froze.

"We'll see about that."

They walked back to their bikes and rode away.

"Don't bother, they just like to show off."

William hoped that's all it was.

They walked for over an hour and stopped when they heard music.

"What the hell?" Norris said, standing in front of the small structure. It looked like a shed. Light fell out of the windows, brightening the surrounding grounds. Inside, William saw a few people.

"It's not supposed to be open."

William frowned. He understood the mental and physical effects of staying indoors too long. It was like living in a comfortable prison. People needed connection; they needed to come together. Socializing was important to everyone.

They entered the pub. It was mostly empty, with just a few folks hanging out in corners. They were far apart from each other. William thought it was acceptable. At least over here, people could maintain a safe distance. In the city, this simple task was hard.

"Hello, Sheriff!" said the bartender.

"Larry. I told you…"

"Oh, come on… I have served nothing for over three months now. I miss it and I think everyone needs it."

Norris looked at the long faces. "Only one night. We have had minimum COVID cases in this county… I would like to keep it that way."

Larry nodded and handed him a drink.

William felt better. The air inside was stale, and the beer didn't taste that good. But it didn't matter. Walking into the pub not only calmed his nervousness, but also made it easy for him to blend in. The people here were friendly and cracked jokes that were out of his league. He was a city boy, and locals here liked to pick on him.

A man entered the pub, and suddenly silence fell. It was a deputy William hadn't met. Norris stood up and faced the man. There was pin-drop silence in the pub. William feared someone else had been murdered.

"Evening, Chief."

"Evening. What's the matter, Kyle?"

The man's eyes surveyed the blank faces. "I think you should it for yourself."

The drive was short, and William's curiosity intensified. The sun was long gone, and a blanket of darkness had fallen over the thick forest. Norris parked on the side of the road and hurriedly stepped out of the truck. William didn't know where he was, and he didn't want to stay alone in the car. He jumped out and came to stand beside the sheriff.

They entered the forest with flashlights. Kyle hadn't uttered a word, and Norris remained speechless. For William, this was alien territory. He was far away from home and wondered if this was a good idea. Roumoult, he trusted with his life. Trust was something that was earned, and although he knew Norris, they had never been in a dangerous situation before. He swallowed hard and prayed for his safety.

As they walked through the forest, it became thicker, darker, and hardly any light penetrated the canopy. Soon the small group stopped, and the flashlights fell on something on the ground. William gulped. It was a deer skinned, alive and half eaten.

"Kyle... it's a dead animal. I don't understand," said Norris.

But William did. He kneeled, observing the twisted neck of the animal and the lacerations on its hind limbs. Under the yellowish glow of the flashlight, he saw what he was afraid of—bite marks. Human bite marks.

21

DARKNESS PREVAILS

15th February 2020 (Present day)
Bridge

I t was colder near the river, and Norris's feet were almost buried in the muddy ground. The wetness penetrated his socks, and he felt a chill run up his spine. He heard a faint thud and turned. Inside the truck, he saw Mrs. Flores. She was sitting up.

"Kyle," he said.

She just sat there, motionless. It was dark, but still Norris could feel her cold eyes on him. Norris slowly set the bag down and placed his hand on the taser.

"What do we do?" Kyle muttered.

"Try not to kill her," replied Norris.

The creature stepped out and stood before them. It growled. In the yellow glow of the headlights, they saw her pale, ghostly skin, and sick eyes. They took a step back.

"Mrs. Flores," warned Norris.

She hissed, taking a step forward.

"Talk to me," Norris said.

She didn't reply. Her hungry eyes remained fixed on them, as if debating which one to attack first. She bared her teeth, screamed, and rushed toward Norris. He reacted and pulled the trigger. A blast of electricity hit Mrs. Flores. She froze, her eyes showing a moment of horror before she fell.

Norris saw the terrified look on Kyle's face. Norris patted him on his shoulder before rushing to the lady and checking her pulse. She was alive, but he doubted her sanity. They carried her and put her in the back seat of the truck again.

"Let's go!" Norris said.

They hurried through the night. The fire was raging and cast an orangish glow in the sky. He wanted to call the fire brigade, but the two firefighters had already turned.

It was freezing, and he could feel his hands go cold. He could hear the water rushing down the creek. Stepping close to the stream, he looked up. The bridge was not too far away.

"This has to work," said Kyle.

Norris sincerely hoped for the best. In order to manage the situation, they had to make sure the villagers don't leave.

Nightridge

Tom stood with his gun pointed toward the door. William was ready. The thudding stopped, and then they heard another boom, causing them to jump.

Silence returned, and he put his gun away. He turned to see the frightened teacher and the children. He grabbed a box, stood on it, and peered out of the window. All he could see was fog.

"They can't stay here any longer," Tom said.

"I know."

"How do we get out of here?" Ms. Pritchard asked.

He cast his eyes over little terrified eyes. A little girl stepped forward and looked at him.

"Please don't leave us," she said.

"Oh, I am so screwed," he thought.

His phone vibrated, and he glanced at a message from Jack: *"Get to the truck. We are running out of time!"*

William sulked. He had hoped to keep the kids out of this, but it was not to be. Now he had to alter his plan.

22

THE SWAM

7th February 2020
County Morgue

William had to step out into the fresh air. He leaned against the stone wall of the building and pondered about Daisy's brain. If he were in the city, he would have called Juliet Wave and others to discuss possibilities. Dr. Wave was one of the Forensic Pathologist who worked with him at the City Morgue. They had been colleagues and friends for the last decade. She was used to his style, and he supported her in all her cases. Until he hadn't come to Nightridge, he hadn't realized how much he relied on her.

With nothing to do, William called it a day and went home.

Meadow Cottage

The morning sun sat far above the horizon, and

although the central heating was on, it struggled to keep the cold at bay. Norris finished his coffee and glanced at his watch. There was no sign of William.

Well, these city boys are lazy, he thought.

He walked to the foot of the stairs, and called out, "William, if you want to join us for a search in the woods, we need to leave soon."

It was half an hour later that William came downstairs looking miserable. He skipped breakfast and yawned. Standing in the kitchen with his shirt half tucked in, he sipped his coffee. Norris knew something was worrying William.

"Morning, you okay?"

"Yeah," William answered unenthusiastically.

A roar of an engine grabbed his attention, and he peered out of the kitchen window to see two trucks.

Soon they were all headed north. Norris kept thinking about the deer in the forest. William was confident it was a human who had attacked and eaten the deer. Norris kept expecting the doc to admit he was wrong, but William remained determined.

Norris wondered about their destination. In order to understand what happened to her, Norris figured it would be a good idea to retrace Daisy's steps.

The sheriff's truck came to a standstill, and the cloud of dust around it settled within seconds. The six deputies and the medical examiner gathered around the truck and studied the map.

They walked at least nine yards away from each other, looking for tracks. They found the campsite within an hour, which was littered with empty cans, chocolate wrappers, and cigarette butts. There were also signs of a fire.

Norris frowned. "Young people value nothing."

It was easy to find Luke's trail. He didn't go that far. Perhaps a few yards to urinate. Daisy was another story. They found her tracks going twice toward the waterfall. At first, it was with Luke, but then it was just her. They followed her trail and Norris wondered how she could walk so far away from the campsite at night. Wasn't she afraid? He remembered Nicholas telling him that the dark didn't scare her.

Her trail took them toward the old caves. It was a structure half buried in the mountains. The opening of the cave led into a small hall with old walls, cracked floor, and was full of foul smells. A home for all kinds of rodents.

Her trail went past the fort, and soon it led to somewhere Norris dreaded. The swamp.

"What was she doing here?" asked William.

"God knows."

"You found no evidence that she crossed the swamp, did you?" asked William.

Norris shook his head. "No one can cross the swamp without a boat."

"What's on the other side?" asked William.

"The mountain. Nothing else."

"Does anyone live on that mountain?" William inquired.

"Not really. There is an abandoned construction site, nothing else," Kyle replied.

They looked at the vast space beyond the stinky swamp.

After an hour, William studied the small boats Norris had arranged.

"Why not a motorboat?"

"The swamp is full of seaweeds and bushes. They would get entangled in the fans of the propeller."

William nodded. He wanted to go with them, but hated the swamp.

"You don't need to come," said Norris.

"Oh, no. I am coming. I am coming," he said while zipping his jacket. He told himself, "I know to swim. So, if I fall, I won't drown."

The three boats left the shore. Hector was rowing the boat, and William and Norris accompanied him.

William was in a strange town with strange people. Being around Norris made William feel better.

"Tell me, doctor, why don't you like the swamp?" Norris asked.

William tried to smile. He looked around. It smelled; the water was dark and looked unnatural. Dead birds and ducks floated over the water. He was sure he saw a snake not too far away.

"It's not... pleasant."

"How many times have you left New York?"

"Oh. Several times..."

"Where did you go?"

"A lot of places."

"But they were all resorts?"

"Ah... sort of."

"I figured."

"I am not an outdoor guy."

The boat rocked, and William grabbed onto the

gunwale. The cops chuckled. He gave a halfhearted smile and tried not to roll his eyes. William suspiciously looked at the water. It was murky, and he couldn't see anything beyond a few centimeters.

The sun was soon to set, and the fog was gathering near the shore and over the water. William shivered despite wearing proper winter clothes. The cops seemed to be calm. On the other hand, William felt uneasy. Back in New York, if he fell or something happened to him, he knew Roumoult or Angelus would come to his aid. Here, all he had was Norris.

The boat shook a bit, and William felt nauseous. His eyes met Norris's, who casually looked away. William turned and peered at the shore. He then eyed the mountain, which looked daunting, unexplored, and yet he was drawn toward it.

"Chief, it's late. We should turn back and come back tomorrow," said Hector.

"Let's keep looking," said Norris.

The three boats moved ahead slowly. They had to use flashlights as the sun was about to set. In the dim light, all they could see were shrubs and bushes sprouting from the water, layers of bags, dirt, and garbage. A strong, pungent smell grabbed William's attention. It was as if someone was burning rubber.

"Do you smell that?" he said.

"Yeah, it's a swamp."

"No. This is different."

William wore gloves and grabbed a small sample bottle.

"Do you really need another sample?" Norris asked.

"Another won't hurt," he said, scooping a bit of water in the sample bottle, sealing it tight.

They got to the edge of the swamp and began turning back. William stared at the dark mountain. The three boats converged on the shore. The dejected men left the boat and started packing up. They had found nothing.

8th February 2020
Meadow Cottage

William looked outside the window, which was dark and dead silent. It was 2 am, and he couldn't sleep. He sat back on his bed and bit his lips. He grabbed his phone and called. To his surprise, Roumoult answered.

"You're awake?"

"So are you," Roumoult responded.

William could see his room was dark, and he was lying on the bed.

"Yeah. I couldn't sleep. What is your excuse?"

"Well, I have nothing to do, and I am living in a madhouse. How is the case?"

"Complex and slow. Waiting for Juliet to finish the tests."

"Anything else?"

"Well, our victim went to a swamp."

Roumoult raised his eyebrows. "Swamp…you mean the shitty place where everything stinks and people get stuck and die."

William tried to control his laughter. "Yeah."

"Anything interesting?"

"No."

"No. Why not?"

"Well, it's just a swamp."

"Did you find any evidence of her entering the swamp?"

"Nothing except some dirt under her nails. But that could be from anywhere."

"Hmm… tell me about the villagers."

"Boring."

Roumoult chuckled. "The big apple has spoiled you."

William rolled his eyes. "I think they are just… simple. The village is so quiet, peaceful, clean, and there is hardly any traffic. They are friendly… yet weird… in a kind of nice way."

"Be careful. The most brutal murders take place in nice quiet villages."

8th February 2020
Meadow Cottage

The sun was up, and Norris came downstairs to his living room and frowned. William was messy. He left his personal stuff around the living room and never washed the dishes. William was untidy and forgot to follow basic hygiene routines like keeping the toilet clean. He glanced at the time; it was already 9 am and William hadn't come downstairs.

After yesterday's walk, Norris took a painkiller. He felt his knee ache, and his muscles were strained. When William didn't wake up, he had breakfast and left.

Sheriff's Office

It was a dull day, and he wasn't finding any more clues. Norris spent a couple of hours going over all the evidence they had collected. It was all in vain.

He got tired and drove to the hospital. On his way, he pulled over when he spotted Ethan and his mother, Mrs. Lark, walking on the roadside.

"Hey," Norris called out.

"Sheriff!" Ethan said excitedly, and reached out to Norris for a hug. Norris tried to stop him. Ethan might carry the contagion, or Norris might be a carrier. Ethan didn't care and hugged him tight. Norris smiled. Ethan was a happy-go-lucky boy, with a big and kind heart, and did odd jobs for all the villagers and studied hard.

"How are you, Mrs. Lark?"

"Very well, thank you," she said. "Just heading home."

"Mom, can I go with the sheriff to watch him solve the new case?"

"No."

Norris laughed. "Ethan, when the lockdown is over we can go hunting."

"But I want to solve the mystery with you."

"In due time," Ethan looked unhappy. "We can go hunting now, can't we?"

Norris smiled. Ethan reminded him of his son, although he was younger. His son was long gone, taken away by the pandemic. Unfortunately, before passing away, the virus targeted his five-year-old grandson. The doctors could do nothing. None of them could be saved. He had lost two sons just in a week.

"We will, soon. Let's deal with the pandemic first."

"Sure. Until then, can I help with the case? Please," Ethan pleaded, "you know, one day I want to be a sheriff... just like you!"

"Ethan..." Mrs. Lark muttered.

"And you will help me? Won't you?" Ethan said.

"Why not? But you must keep your promise and finish school."

"I will! I will!" said Ethan excitedly.

Norris laughed.

Local Hospital

Meeting young people like Ethan gave him hope and joy. It showed him there was goodness in the world, despite all the evil.

He spoke with Nicholas's doctor, and they were positive that he could completely recover physically, but his mental status remained a major concern. He said Nicholas had become really quiet, distant, and could be mentally disturbed. The doctor had put him on antidepressants.

Norris walked in and Nicholas looked at him with sad eyes.

"Hello Nicholas, how are you?"

Nicholas said nothing, but looked at him with hollow eyes.

People are so vulnerable, and life is so short.

"How are you?" he asked again.

"Fine."

For a while, they chatted about the past, their child-hood, and how they used to play in the fields and catch butterflies. They laughed, remembering they had a crush on the same girl in school. When they became silent, Norris asked a question.

"I wanted to know, would Daisy would go into the swamp?"

"No. No. She would never go there!"

Sheriff's Office

Norris returned to the office and started going through the girl's phone. On it, he found some notes. Most of them were about her studies. He found notes on history, science and math. He kept flipping, but suddenly came to a stop. A few words sparked his imagination. He read the words again and again.

"What is in the swamp?"

In the next few hours, Norris, William, and other cops assembled near the swamp. Today William looked more settled, and they left shore immediately.

The three boats moved east, between the mountain and the swamp. The sheriff nodded, and the deputy lowered the black pipe underneath the murky water. They all stared at a small monitor. Th blackness, dirt, seaweeds, and years of rubbish didn't surprise Norris.

I should get this cleaned, he thought.

Only one boat was equipped with a camera. On each of two other boats was a diver and two deputies. The diver was ready to retrieve evidence, and the cops waited to help.

Norris thought there would be more resistance to such an activity. In the past four months, people had been forced to stay indoors and had lost opportunities to explore the world. Human beings were meant for adventure, and even though this was a rancid job, the team was happy to do it.

Norris knew one man who would not be happy, the mayor. He didn't care. He felt the swamp had something to do with Daisy's death. The boat rocked a bit, and his eyes turned to the monitor.

William watched the screen keenly. Norris admired his spirit, and he was doing well for a city boy. He wished William was more organized, but then recalled his son was no different. The pain in his chest returned, and he slowly pushed away the feelings of remorse.

The boat shifted again, and the monitor turned blurry.

"What happened?" Norris asked.

"We hit something."

The paddling stopped, and screen turned black. He felt as if they were staring into a void. The men remained patient, and soon the soil settled. Something shone in the darkness, and as the murky water settled, a whitish object became visible.

"It's just a cylinder?" said Hector.

"What is it doing here?" asked William.

The cops shook their heads.

"Could we get it?" William asked.

The cops exchanged glances.

One diver slowly got into the water. The water rose to his neck, and then he disappeared underneath.

After a while, he emerged with the cylinder. The others grabbed it and slowly placed it on the boat. The diver swam toward his boat.

The thin, 70-inch-long cylinder sat in the middle of four men.

"Is it heavy?"

"No. Probably empty."

Wearing gloves, Norris watched the medical examiner clear the dirt on the metal.

"Does anyone around here use cylinders like these?" William asked.

All shook their heads no.

Norris didn't like it. He picked up the radio. "Has anyone seen white cylinders in the swamp. Over."

"No. Over."

"Okay. Keep looking. Over." He put the radio away. "Tell me, William, could this be dangerous?"

"I don't know. It looks like a standard cylinder. What is it doing here?"

Norris shrugged his shoulders.

They kept looking. The rowing was almost rhythmic. They searched five kms radius on both sides.

As the afternoon dawned, Norris became jaded. He was getting old. While the others stared at the monitor, he set his eyes on the unexplored mountain.

The three boats were now heading east. They had already covered a lot of area, and Norris wondered if he should call it a day. But he wanted to be sure that there was nothing here that had sealed Daisy's fate.

"Stop," called William.

The rhythm of the paddling broke.

"I think there is something down there."

Norris came to his side and peered into the monitor. They waited for the soil below to settle as much as it could. The seaweeds swayed, and a school of fish rushed past cameras. They waited. From the corner of his eye, he saw a diamondback water snake. He had seen several in the swamp and also in the forest. His deputies didn't look alarmed, but he could see the terror in William's eyes.

"It's harmless," Norris said.

"What are we looking for?" asked Hector.

"That…" William replied, pointing to a heap of soil. "Why does it look different?"

Norris had to focus; his eyesight was not as good. The soil underneath was almost flat, murky, but in one area it appeared to be elevated.

There was excitement on the boat, and the diver got into the water. All eyes turned toward the monitor. Soon the diver came into vision and slowly cleared the dirt.

"Chief, it's just a heap of filth," said Hector.

Norris spoke into the radio. "Take it slow. Be careful."

"Roger that," replied the diver.

Every minute passed slowly, and the feed was fuzzy.

"It's filthy, sticky, and I don't want to know what it smells like," remarked the diver.

"Be careful now," said Norris.

The diver finished clearing a part of the section.

"Stop!" William shouted.

Everyone jumped.

"Sorry. Do you see that?"

Norris peered in, and within the murkiness, he could see a round object. "What is it?"

"A head," William replied.

23

BRAVE SCOUTS

15th February 2020 (Present day)
Bridge

As they stood glaring at the enormous structure, Kyle asked Norris. "Are you sure?"

"I have to try," Norris said looking up and down the river. It was gloomy, and the noise of the raging water muffled their voices.

What choice did they have? There was no coming coming to help. The world was plagued. Fear and darkness ruled people's minds. He felt like dropping the bag himself, punching Kyle in his face and vanishing into the darkness. He knew he could never do that. Norris could never live with himself. He couldn't abandon this world even after it had taken everything from him.

Trying to fight the cold, he rubbed his hands together. Kyle unzipped the bag and revealed its contents. Norris's heart jumped a beat. Kyle slowly began putting the C4 together.

Norris observed the bridge, trying to figure out the best way they could do it. He knew once the bridge was gone; they were trapped with a mob of maniacs and may not survive the night. On the other hand, If William's plan worked, everything should be okay. Norris chest stuttered, and he told himself it was going to be okay.

Nightridge

Trapped in the old basement of the school, William felt his dread rise.

"Are you sure?" he asked, hoping he had heard wrong.

"Yes," said Jack from the other end of the line. "From what I can see, they are about three to four blocks North East. You need to get out now!"

William ended the call. His phone beeped, notifying him only ten percent of the battery was left.

"So?" Tom asked.

"We have no choice," muttered William. "If we want to implement my plan, we can't stay here. But we can't leave them."

William nodded toward Mrs. Pritchard. She sulked and kneeled, and the children gathered around her.

"Scouts, you have been so brave," she said. "It's time to get out of here. Do you understand?"

The little heads nodded with uncertainty.

"Great. You remember the fire drill?"

The children nodded.

"Is there a fire?" inquired one kid.

Ms. Pritchard gulped.

"Yes. A big one," replied William.

"Is it because of the fire everyone is screaming?"

"Yes… they are scared. Just like we are," replied William.

"Why don't they hide? Like us?" asked another child.

The adults exchanged worried glances.

"There is not enough space," answered Tom, clearly lying.

The children looked confused.

"But now," said Ms. Pritchard, "we need to leave."

"Why?"

"Because the is spreading and we must get to safety."

"And we need your help," said William.

The children glanced at each other.

"We might be kids, but we are not stupid. You want to get us out of here because it's not safe anymore."

"And we know everyone has gone crazy," added another.

William looked at Tom and said, "Remind me never to make up stories for my kids."

"I want my mommy," cried a girl who was clearly younger than others.

"I told you, Cassey. It's going to be okay," said another child.

Everyone became silent.

"Remember the fire drill. Hold your partner's hand, stay together, do not leave the group, and you have to be really quiet," said Ms. Pritchard. "Now, do you understand?"

The children looked alarmed, but they nodded.

"Okay. Listen. We have to get to a house. You will have to walk really fast… do you understand?" William said.

"Again, we are not stupid," said a kid.

William stood up to look at Tom's smiling face.

"Shut up," William muttered.

"Are you ready?" asked Ms. Pritchard.

All heads nodded.

William moved back as the children formed a line. They held their partners' hands and waited.

Tom was about to lead, but William grabbed his arm.

"I will go first," William said.

"Are you nuts? There might be someone out there."

"Yes, if I am caught or taken… at least they have you to protect them."

"Roumoult is going to kill me," muttered Tom as William walked past him toward the door. He glanced behind at the group and prayed that everything goes as planned.

24

LADY IN THE SWAMP

8ᵗʰ February 2020
The Swamp

The sun was disappearing behind the mountain as two divers carefully uncovered the body. The men waited in silence. As they cleared months or what could be years of muck, they found two cement slabs with chains had been used to bog the body down. It was tedious and slow work, and the drop in temperature wasn't helping. It surprised Norris to see William get into a diver's suit and enter the water to make sure the body was safe to move.

The men carefully brought the corpse to the surface. Her eyes were closed, and her face was half eaten. Her skin was pasty white, and a large wound on her stomach had turned black. She wore no shoes, and a torn ivory dress stuck to her fragile body. Her hair was tangled with seaweed.

Grief clouded his mind as Norris's boat neared the

shore. He wanted to know why Daisy died, and now he had found another woman. From the condition of the body, it was apparent she died a long time ago. Yet, he was not an expert and had to wait for William's report.

Everyone looked miserable. They had daughters, wives and mothers. Everyone had someone to lose. The boat touched the shore, and all got off except Norris.

"Sheriff?" asked William.

"You guys go ahead. I wanted to check something."

Hector approached the boat.

"No, I need to do this alone."

"That's a bad idea. What if something happens?" said William.

All eyes turned to William. His men never argued with him, but William wasn't one of them.

"I will be fine," Norris said.

Norris was a loner. He didn't like crowds and people questioning his motives. He liked peace, silence, and he preferred to do things in a certain way.

The sky was clear, and the wind chilly. He rowed the boat slowly, admiring the dark surroundings. There were snakes, alligators and years of garbage just a few inches below, but it didn't bother him.

He secretly wondered, "What did Daisy see?"

The Swamp

By the time he reached the foot of the mountain, Norris was exhausted. He left the boat and hiked. After half an hour, he stopped to admire the open sea. He could hardly see the ocean because of the heavy fog. He checked his flashlight and his radio and kept walking.

The hike was pleasant, and he wanted to lose himself in the peaceful mountain. Besides, that was not what had drawn him toward it. While they were searching the swamp, he thought he had seen something on the mountain. Was it a vehicle? An animal? A man? He didn't know. He was just following his instinct.

After half an hour of walking, he started feeling as if he had made a mistake. It was dark, and he had already seen two wild boars. He turned and watched the open sea. The wind was chilly, and a thick fog had spread all over the mountain.

Shaking his head, thinking it was all for nothing, he turned back. He was about to get in the boat when he heard a thud. He froze. The ground shook a little, and the water vibrated. Startled, he looked back and forth. He saw nothing but haze. It was quiet again, as if it never happened.

9th February 2020
County Morgue

William felt excited. He had something to do before returning to Daisy's brain. Juliet still had to call him back. For now, he could focus on the second body. He had realized that if he was free; he kept thinking about those unidentified objects. Wholeheartedly, he wished they were just anomalies.

He began with his primary examination. The cause of death was apparent, which was a gunshot wound in her stomach. Probably two shots. Close range. Any gunshot residue would have been washed away years ago.

Fredrick arrived, followed by the postman.

"You have a delivery," said the postman and dropped the hefty box on the floor.

"Oh, thanks. Just leave it there. That should be the scanner."

Fredrick eyed him, and William wondered if he was going to ask him about the scanner. Instead, he calmly got ready for another autopsy.

While William photographed every inch of the body, Fredrick began taking samples.

Soon they rolled the body toward the X-ray room. To his surprise, the radiologist on call came sooner than he expected.

William couldn't believe how much time every process took. Yet he enjoyed it. He felt like he was back at the academy.

The room was bare, except for the X-ray machine. He watched Dr. Gaber do his work. A skinny older man who wore a loose apron and enormous glasses. He looked as if hadn't slept or spoken for years.

The body lay under the thin white blanket on a cold steel bed. Angling the head upwards, he went back to the machine and pushed the button. It produced a loud noise and then became silent. The chest was next. The radiologist moved the bulky head of the machine downward and stopped at her chest, then pushed the button. Step by step, he scanned every aspect of the body.

Once the X-rays were done, Fredrick rolled the body back to the autopsy room.

By the time the X-rays developed, they continued taking samples. William spent a few minutes looking at the sample of her hair follicle underneath the microscope. The door opened with a bang. William jumped. The radiologist walked in, handed him the films, and walked out.

"Well, good night," William muttered.

Fredrick shrugged. "Yeah, he is like that."

William rolled his eyes and threw the report aside. He placed the film on the viewer and turned the light on. It was her right leg. He couldn't see any fractures, contusions, or anything that would ring a bell. The hands and head X-rays were clear. He put up the last scan. The victim's chest lit up, and he froze. He heard Fredrick gasp. His face moved closer to the display. Between the diaphragm disappearing beyond the soft tissues, he could see a blackish object.

"What the hell is that?" Fredrick asked.

William shut his eyes.

County Morgue

Norris was tired, and last night's events bothered him. Not wanting to do any more paperwork, he decided to pay William a visit. It served another purpose. He wanted to know about the woman in the swamp. He entered the morgue, walked down the narrow passageway, and pushed open the door. The unknown woman's body was cut open and William's hands were deep inside her. He had a quizzed look on his face. Nausea took over Norris.

"Hey," William said.

Norris nodded as his eyes settled over a bundle of body parts lying between the legs of the bare body.

"What are you doing?" he said, offended. In his eyes, the dead should be treated with respect.

"Trying to find something," William answered, pulling out a body part which looked like a string of muscle.

"What is that?" he asked, feeling his stomach twitch.

"The gut."

"Why are you pulling out her guts?"

"To find the stomach…"

Norris knew he was going to regret this. "Why?"

"There is something in it. And it's not seaweed."

Norris was shocked. He watched as William pulled out a whitish bag and slowly sliced it open. Looking away, Norris shut his eyes. But then curiosity took over, and he watched William dig into the bag with his fingers.

"Ah! Got it!" he said excitedly.

Norris stepped forward, feeling a sense of shock and confusion. William looked equally confused. Both men studied the USB drive in William's hand.

Meadow Cottage

Although William wanted to continue working, fatigue was something he couldn't fight. He got a copy of her fingerprints and then headed home with the sheriff. He showered, welcoming the warm, clean water as it eliminated traces of the swamp and the smell of formaldehyde. After getting changed in his room, he soon came down to the kitchen. Tonight, he thought he should make dinner.

Norris seemed happy when someone else cooked and

looked satisfied with the simple yet greasy food. William hoped he had cooked the steaks well and also roasted some potatoes. He hoped it was enough.

They ate quietly, until William asked, "Why did you go back?"

Norris looked calm, as if expecting the question. "I had a feeling there was something there."

"Did you find anything?"

"I don't know."

10th February 2020

It was after midnight when they finished their dishes and cleaned the kitchen. They said their goodnights, and William returned to his room. Since he couldn't sleep, he called Detective Tom Nash, studying studied the paper in front of him.

Tom took his time to answer. When the video call connected, all William could see was darkness. He heard a loud bang, and the lights came on. Tom was awkwardly dressed, wearing a thick armor-like suit and a black helmet. It was apparent the detective had just returned home.

"Hey. What's up? Haven't heard from you for a while," Tom said breathlessly.

William was afraid to ask.

At the moment, the issues faced by the law enforcement agencies were drastic and volatile. William didn't think that corrupt cops or people getting away with murder in broad daylight was right, but he felt he had very little say in it. The problem was that good detectives like Tom suffered because of the unacceptable behavior of a few cops. Then there was the pandemic. Maintaining order during a time of chaos was a challenge.

"You, okay?" William asked, looking at Tom's pale expression. He watched him reach for a bottle of sanitizer and rub it in.

"Yeah. I am good. Good... fine... just fine."

Tom picked what looked like an air freshener. William knew it wasn't. With the widespread pandemic, aerosol sanitizers were pretty common. He watched Tom spray it all over himself and then around the apartment.

"What are you doing?"

"Sanitizing."

"Yeah. It would kill everything, including you! Stop!"

Tom looked offended. "I am just being cautious."

"I know. Sorry. Where have you been? What's with the armor?"

The detective looked gloomy. "They called us in to control the riots," he said, removing the armor.

"Oh. I see. How did it go?"

He gave him a look. "I don't know what's wrong with this world. It's crazy. People... are not people any more..."

"That happens when economies shut down."

"It's not right. It's not right," Tom stated sadly. "We don't know how long we can stay in control or perhaps... letting go might be a good idea. No one knows what's going to happen. No one! The world is going to end!"

William remained quiet.

"I miss the good old days. Solving murders, catching bad guys, and doing what felt right. This is wrong. I want everything to go back to as it was. I want everything to return to normal."

William bit his tongue. Unfortunately, controlling a mutating virus was a challenge. He knew nothing will ever be the same. Just like every plague, this one would leave its mark on human history and change the world forever.

"You are not in the city?" said Tom, studying the background. "Great. Roumoult is in Canada, Angelus in Mexico, and you are god knows where! I am stuck here in this hellhole!"

Angelus was a dear friend and a private detective who was working on a case in Mexico when the pandemic hit. The boarders closed, and William assumed he was still there. It bothered him that no one had heard from Angelus.

"Trust me, everyone is right now in their own kind of hell. Roumoult is on a ranch."

Tom froze. "A ranch?"

"Yep. They had to move. He is locked in a house with six kids, an old couple, his father and god knows how many animals."

"Oh, I see. Have you heard from Angelus?"

"No. He'll return when he can."

Tom nodded. "I could use some good company."

"You are alone? Is Jenny in the UK?"

"Yep. Where are you?"

"I came down to Nightridge to help Sheriff Cunningham."

Tom raised an eyebrow. "Good. Good. So, what's the case?"

"Yeah," William muttered.

"Tell me about it."

William updated him briefly, mentioning the body from the swamp, Daisy's murder, and the USB discovery.

"Wow! That is something."

"Don't tell Roumoult."

"We are keeping Roumoult out of this?"

"For as long as we can."

"Why?"

"You know how he is. Once he starts solving a puzzle, he won't stop. I think he needs time to recover."

"Yeah? Okay, you got a deal."

"We found another body in the swamp."

"Of course," Tom muttered sarcastically.

"Can you help me identify her? I can email you her fingerprints."

"Sure. I'll do anything to forget about this stupid pandemic!"

William couldn't sleep. He watched the stars from his window. Man, they were beautiful and so many. Never had he seen such a stunning sight from his apartment in the city.

Amongst many things, in the shadow of the pandemic, true fears of people were being revealed. His biggest concern was not to be loved by the person he loved. He called Joan several times, but she didn't pick up. Something felt off. He didn't know if it was him or if it was her.

He was a bit jealous of Roumoult and his girlfriend Emma. Emma was expressive, poured her heart out and told Roumoult everything. Sometimes too much. But Roumoult was happy with that.

Joan was different. If she wasn't happy with something, she would completely shut down. She became silent, reserved. Unfortunately, he was the same.

10th February 2020

William only slept for a couple of hours, and he woke up before the sun rose. The rooster crowed, and he could hear the birds singing. He took a shower, checked his emails, and then went straight to the kitchen.

Coffee was brewing when he heard the sheriff come down the stairs.

"Ah, you are up early today."

William glanced back and smiled. "Good morning. Do you want some?" he asked, pointing toward the eggs.

They ate breakfast and enjoyed the coffee. William made a note to go to the supermarket and get some groceries. He didn't want to be a burden on Norris. Of course, he was a guest, but it had been a week since he had arrived. His thoughts were interrupted when his phone rang; it was Tom.

"Hey, morning."

"Morning. I have emailed you the results," said Tom.

"That was quick."

"Oh, trust me, it is the only exciting thing I have done for weeks."

"What did you find?"

"The prints belong to a Ms. Lauren Kin, a reporter that worked for *New York Post* and a freelancer for an environmental magazine called *Our Earth*. She went missing six months ago."

"Really?"

"Yeah."

"Any idea what she was working on?"

"I called the editor, and he said the last thing he knew she was writing a piece on the environmental changes occurring in the water in northeast New York. She was targeting several water bodies, including the ones in Nightridge. She never finished her research or the article because she vanished."

"And no one cared?"

"When they didn't hear from her, the parents called the cops. The cops filed a missing person report, conducted a search, but found nothing. They interviewed the ex-husband, her friends and the last man she had dated and came up empty-handed."

"Hmm."

"She lived alone in New Jersey. She was divorced and had no kids. I went through the officer's report. He did a thorough job. He interviewed several people. They all said she kept to herself, shared little, and was career-driven. It could be due to her divorce. It was finalized eight months before her disappearance. According to her parents, she never recovered. She started working longer and harder. The man she dated, Daniel Wake, was the first date she had been to in months."

"What about Daniel?"

"Nothing. Just a straightforward accountant who likes crosswords."

"Interesting."

"Indeed. What's the COD?"

"Looks like a gunshot wound. I recovered two 38-caliber bullets yesterday."

"Can you pinpoint the time of death?"

"My estimation is around the same time she vanished."

"Okay. Keep me posted."

"Will do."

County Morgue

After wearing protective gloves, William picked up the USB. He had noticed yesterday that it was coated with a plastic sheet. He had cautiously removed it, cleaned it with a dry tissue, and left it overnight to dry.

Today, he cleaned the device once more with antiseptic tissue. The exterior didn't look damaged. He walked to the PC and plugged it into the computer and waited. Nothing happened. He removed it and plugged it again.

"Damn!" he said.

He didn't want to do it, but now he had no option. He had not one, but two, reasons to get Jack involved. William glanced at his watch and wondered what time it was in California.

Murphy's Home

After dropping the doc at the morgue, Norris went straight to Murphy's house. He felt he had missed something. The doctors were considering releasing Nicholas, and Norris thought that was a bad idea. He was better at the hospital. At home, he would be alone and the death of his family would haunt him.

Nicholas was a happy-go-lucky person, but that was

before this tragedy. Norris had never seen Nicholas angry, or ever complain about anything. Now there was something different about him. The doctors thought it was shock or PTSD. But Norris believed it was something else. He had changed, somehow. For the first few days after the death of his family, Nicholas sobbed, and he wanted answers. That was natural, and it was a situation Norris had faced several times. Yet during the last two visits, Nicholas was more distant than ever. He remained quiet and just stared out of the window. He hardly answered questions, nor did he ask how the investigation was going. As if he was in the world of his own.

Inside the house, he memories of the day of the murder. At first, it was just two dead women. Now they had found a third one. The reporter's death may not be related to Daisy and her mother, but it was Daisy's trail that had led them to the swamp.

Wearing his gloves, he walked around the house. The kitchen was untouched, the bedroom carpet cut out and taken in by forensics. He searched the study. He didn't know what he was looking for. The books were mostly on traveling and cooking. He went through the drawers in the study, found a few deeds, bills and reports about the timber mill. Nothing astonishing. It was all business-related.

Daisy's room was a different place, and as he searched the drawers, he found a dairy. He felt uncomfortable reading a dead girl's diary. On the other hand, he needed answers.

The diary was full of a teenage girl's fantasies, her life at school, at home, her friends, and most of it was about herself and her boyfriend. Norris closed the book and sighed. He went to the closet and began checking for clues. He found some boxes, which were full of toys and old books. Nothing exciting. He checked under the bed and the mattress. He was about to leave when he heard something crack under his feet. Looking down at the ground, he realized that there was no carpet in this room. He got on his knees and pushed his hand against the floor. The panel moved. Using his fingertips, he opened the section of the floor. Inside, he found a smartphone.

He sat patiently on the floor as the phone turned on, and the first thing he saw was Daisy's smiling face. He read through all the text messages and felt uncomfortable. Looking into someone's personal life was not something he liked. As he scrolled, he found a few videos of the teenagers getting wasted and dancing around the pool. It could have been last summer.

The good old days, he thought.

Then he watched a two videos of a bunch of girls, including Daisy, singing in the forest.

He ignored them. Then his attention was drawn toward the photo gallery. He found some pictures of the mountain on the night Daisy was out with Luke. He flicked through the pictures. They were blurry and dark, but Norris could make out the mountain edges under the moonlight. Suddenly, he stopped and flipped back. It was the section of the mountain facing east. His breath left him when he realized what Daisy must have seen. The mountain had moved.

25

MIND YOUR STEP

15th February 2020 (Present day)
Bridge

The water rushed below the bridge. Norris could feel his heart pound in his chest.

"Let me do it," said Kyle.

"No. I should do it."

Kyle nodded warily.

Without another word, Norris climbed the steel ladder. It was cold and slippery. He tried to hold on and slowly made the climb. The bomb's bag hung over his back as he reached the top of the ladder.

He observed the narrow scaffold attached to the pillar. If he slipped, it was a long fall. But he had little choice. Grabbing the lower part of the bridge, he stretched his leg. The tip of his shoe barely touched the scaffold. Taking a deep breath, he swayed from the ladder, setting his foot on the cold platform. Using the lower part of the bridge, he pushed himself over. He quickly gripped the pillar of the bridge for support. Breathing slowly, trying not to freak out, he began moving along the pillar.

The water rushed under the bridge; waves crashed against its pillars. Thick mist surrounded Norris, and he could barely see anything. Gradually he moved along the curved narrow platform of the bridge. His heart was beating fast, and he struggled to breathe. The wind picked up, and he felt a chill down his spine. He spotted a narrow steel walkway that stretched along the bridge. Slowly, he reached out and grabbed the metal bar with one hand. He quickly got on the walkway. Taking a deep breath, he took a step forward. His foot slipped, and he fell.

"Chief!" Kyle shouted.

Nightridge

The door cracked open, and William peeped out. The air was full of alcohol, urine, and death. He moved forward and looked up the stairs. The door to the basement was open. He gripped the gun tightly and made his way up the stairs.

Taking a deep breath, he peeped. Lights blinked intermittently. Paper, empty cans, bottles, and broken furniture covered the floor.

He looked over his shoulder and nodded, then tiptoed down the corridor. The small group followed him. He paused again and observed the main door was half open.

"Move," he told himself.

He rushed toward the door. Tom followed him. The children began talking but were hushed by Ms. Pritchard.

Fredrick stood at the end, glancing up and down the corridor.

William peered through the half glass doors and saw nothing. It was gloomy and a rattling noise filled the air. He froze and waited. The street was empty and still. Fog drifted along with the cold air, and the cars parked silently in the street.

When he thought it was safe, he signaled Tom to stay put and gradually opened the door. The town hall bell sounded and then fell silent. He had a bad feeling that someone was out here. Closing the door, he tiptoed down the stairs and rushed to the school gates. He kneeled and looked around. There was not a soul in sight. He waited, trying to listen. Nothing. Thinking that it was safe enough, he turned. He almost screamed when an icy hand grabbed his neck and a set of horrifying eyes glared at him.

26

SPIDERS NEST

10th February 2020
County Morgue

William checked the photographic evidence. Once he was happy with it, he put it in a file and put it aside. The two 38-caliber bullets gave him nothing. Such guns were very common; hard to trace and easy to lose. He made a note of his ballistic finding', and he carefully packed the bullets. Perhaps the gun was used in a previous crime, and they might have the ballistic reports in the system. If he was really lucky, they could catch a break.

He didn't need Juliet to tell him what killed Lauren. Fredrick had received her primary tests. They were negative.

He thought the murder weapon might still be in the swamp. But it would be impossible to locate. Except for the USB, he had nothing. It was a long shot; Lauren's murderer may never be found. He remembered a cabinet in his office. It was full of unsolved murders, cases that remain open due to lack of evidence. Several dead men and women who had taken their secrets to their graves.

His phone buzzed. He pushed the green button. The screen came to life, and Jack was smiling at him.

"Hey, looks like you are right where I left you!"

"Ha ha, hilarious," William answered, remembering the evening when they last spoke. It was a similar day, but he was working on the pandemic case, not a murder case.

"Dude, how are you?"

"I am fine. How about you?"

"I am alright," said Jack. "My job is done. But Boss doesn't want me to return."

"It's safer for you and Alice. Stay in California, for now."

"We miss home."

"Don't worry, things will get back to normal."

"Will they?"

William changed the topic. "Okay. I need you."

"Of course, you only call when you need me."

William shut his eyes. "Sorry, I was just in a bad place," he answered, remembering his experience in the hospital.

Jack looked unhappy. "I know. The only thing that keeps me cheery is Alice."

William bowed.

Clapping his hands together, Jack said, "Okay. What do you need me to do?"

"Get data of a USB drive."

Jack's face fell. "Are you kidding me? That's it? A bloody USB drive!"

William wanted to tell him about the unidentified objects, but he hesitated. "The USB is not working."

"Still, you could have got me something more exciting!"

"Jack!"

"Fine. Fine. What happened to it?"

"Let's say it has been in a very unhygienic place."

Jack raised his eyebrows.

William was never daunted so much in his life. He felt if he made a mistake, he would lose something valuable. Like codes to a nuclear bomb. He took in a deep breath.

"Don't worry... you won't do anything wrong. You allowed it to dry, right?"

"Yes," William said.

"Okay. I need to see inside."

He slowly opened the cover. Inside he saw a light green circuit board, with a small and a large black square.

"Okay, the connector looks okay. Can you zoom in on the circuit board?"

"Yeah sure." William grabbed the phone and held it near the drive.

"This looks promising. The mass storage controller looks okay, but the flash memory chip looks a little bad."

"Memory? That is what we need right."

"Bring the camera closer."

William did as he was told and waited. He wished he could send it over to Jack.

"Looks like there has been some damage, but I might get you what you want."

"How?"

William's hand shook a little as he handled the micro-soldering gun. It had taken them an hour to find it. He had called Norris, who had contacted the local electrician and Fredrick, and drove to the electrician home to pick it up.

"Take care…" Jack warned.

"I am doing my best…" William said, shutting his eyes for a second.

The USB was under his microscope and Jack had told him that the connection of the memory chip had severed from the circuit board. He had already used flux and cleaned the surface as much as possible. Now he had to solder them to the board one by one. This may or may not work. With shaking hands, he soldered the first circuit, and then the second one. As time passed by, he imagined performing surgery on a lifeless thing that contained important data. This thought made it easier.

Once it was done, they waited. On Jack's instructions, he tried the USB again.

"Yes! It works," he said joyfully. "Let me see if the files open… hopefully they are not corrupted."

"William, as soon as you open a file, print it or save it on the PC. There is no guarantee how long the USB will work."

He saw an unnamed folder on the USB. When he opened the folder, he saw several files and opened the first one. The screen flickered for a second and then a graph came into view. He didn't think and hit the print button. Then he opened the next one and found another graph. It looked similar to the previous one, but he wanted to be sure, so he printed it. Most of the files were charts, and he made copies of them all. Several were corrupted. The last two files were pictures. The first one was of cylinders, which looked like the ones they found in the swamp.

William opened the last photo. "What the hell is this?"

He printed the photo and observed the creature. The multiple eyes glared at him; its legs appeared as if trying to reach out of the picture. The spider wasn't anything like he had seen before.

While William tried to find a pattern in the graphs, Jack tried to find out about the spider. The door opened, and Norris rushed toward him.

"What do you make of this?" Norris asked, giving him a mobile.

William glanced at the terrified cop and then focused on the phone. He glared at the picture of the mountain and flipped to the next one. At first, he didn't get it, but soon he understood.

"There is something on that mountain," Norris muttered.

William left Norris with his puzzle and focused on the clues in front of him. A daughter who killed the mother and attacked the father for no reason. The mother's over-possessive behavior might have been a trigger, but was it enough to kill? Then there were the unidentified objects. He had spent an hour on the internet trying to find something similar; it was all in vain. In his career as a medical examiner, wives killing husbands, and vice versa, were common. Revenge was a powerful motive, so was jealousy. But what was the motive here? He couldn't do anything until he had dissected the brain and examined the anomalies. He checked the refrigerator and felt happy. Soon, he could return to solving the mystery of Daisy's death.

The next mystery was the journalist. Surely she knew something. The cause of death was apparent, but then the culprits hid her body in the swamp using cement slabs. He had checked; they belong to a local cement factory about ten miles away. From what Norris had told him, it was locked, and anyone could have stolen them. It was a clue, but not a clue that could narrow down the suspect list.

The USB was interesting. Surely it was important for her to swallow it. She knew she was going to die, but she didn't know that it would take six months for her body to be found, and that too by chance.

By the afternoon, William had returned to Daisy's brain. The smell of formalin was giving him a headache, and his mask or shield wasn't helping.

He turned toward the MRI. The unidentified objects were at the base of the brain, near the hippocampus. He gradually turned the brain and picked up the blade and made an incision to separate the brain stem.

In a few minutes, he held the brain stem and the cerebellum. Carefully, he sliced through the organ and cut it in half. His heart jumped a beat. There in the sticky, spongy tissue he saw it. It was tiny, black, elongated, and he was afraid of it. One thing he knew, it wasn't organic.

What was it? What secrets did it hold? he thought.

His hand shook as he grabbed a sterile tweezer. He slowly separated it from its surrounding, put it in a small container, and sealed it tight.

He turned his attention to find the next object. Referring to the MRI images, he estimated the next one should be just a few centimeters deeper. He made another slice and found the second one.

Separating it from the tissue, he deposited it in a second container. The third one was near the base of the brain stem. He carefully removed the anomaly and put it in the third container. Once all inside, he observed the three objects in the containers and wondered what to do next.

"What were they? How did they get into her brain? Who put them there?"

Not allowing himself to get overwhelmed, he prepared standard brain samples to be sent to Juliet ASAP. Of course, he could do them on his own, but the facilities over here were limited, and he didn't want to get anyone else involved. He didn't know who he could trust.

William worked fast and sent the samples to the pathologist before the post office closed. Then he returned to the morgue feeling a mix of dread and curiosity.

He wore protective gear and began again. Once it was separated from the brain tissue, he had an unobstructed view of the object. He inspected it under the microscope. It had a shell and was about one centimeter long with two short arms. It had no striations on its outer surface, but he observed something. There was a fine line right in the middle of the object.

Could it be? he thought.

He carefully turned it over and increased the magnification, noticing a mark. A small imprint. Pointed ends of three drops came together to form an inverted triangle. It was a logo.

Magnifying the logo, he grabbed his mobile and took a

picture. He forwarded it to Jack and the sheriff. Maybe one of them could help him identify it.

He returned to the microscope, and the object sat right where he had left it. He picked up the slide and placed it on the table. With extreme care, he slit through the fine line. It split opened without resistance, almost like jelly. He cautiously settled it back on a slide and then observed it under the microscope. His jaw dropped. Its interior was full of tiny circuits. He moved away, and his hands shivered. This was not what he had expected. What was it? What did it do, and how did it enter her body?

Meadow Cottage

The clock struck 9 pm, and William removed the gloves. He was done for the day, and he needed fresh air. He had thought uncovering the objects would give him more answers, instead it had raised more questions.

He walked home with his hands in his pockets. He was jaded and couldn't think straight.

The fresh, cool air was welcoming instead of the stink of formaldehyde. William had two missed calls from Joan, but he didn't want to call her back. He stopped when he thought he heard a rustle. Thinking it was probably an animal, he walked toward the house.

Using his keys, William let himself in. It was dark upstairs, Norris had probably gone to bed. He turned the lights on in the kitchen. He almost jumped when he saw Norris sitting on the enormous chair with a glass of whisky.

"Hiya," Norris said.

"Why are you sitting in the dark?"

"It helps me think. Also, I couldn't sleep and noticed you hadn't returned. I was about to check on you."

"Thanks. Did you eat?"

Norris nodded. "Your dinner is in the fridge."

"Thanks," William replied, opening the fridge.

William was grateful for the company, and for some time, they spoke about things unrelated to the case. Since he was eager to know his next step, William asked, "So, what do you plan to do about the mountain?"

"I don't know what I can do. But I am sure it has something to do with Daisy's death."

"I think the journalist died because she thought something was going on in the swamp."

"Here is my question. Why did she suspect in the first place?" asked Norris. "What brought her here?"

11th February 2020
The Swamp

The sun was up, and Norris stood at the edge, staring over the water. It was quieter today, and fog still covered most of the regions of the mountain. Along with his deputies, including Kyle and Hector, he was all set to go toward the mountain. They heard footsteps, and Ethan emerged from the thick forest.

"Good morning, everyone!" he said excitedly.

"What are you doing here?" asked Norris.

"I called the Sheriff's office and Mrs. Flores said that you were heading to the mountain to investigate a clue. Can I come, please? Please, please, please."

The deputies smiled. Everyone liked Ethan.

"No," Norris said.

"Oh, come 'on Chief," said Kyle.

"No. It could get dangerous."

"As long as he doesn't wander off on his own, I don't see a problem," said Mathews.

Ethan nodded enthusiastically. "I won't. I promise."

Norris was about to say no, but he looked into those innocent eyes of Ethan. The boy reminded him too much of his own son.

"Okay. Fine. Stay with me, okay?"

Ethan smiled and got in the boat.

The three boats rowed slowly toward the mountain. Norris had assigned one man on the boat to use the camera and two men to keep an eye on the monitor. They seemed to be over enthusiastic to do their job today. The body in the swamp had raised hopes.

With his senses on total alert, he listened to every sound. Most of it was birds singing and ducks quacking. Ethan remained quiet, attentive. The rhythmic splashes of the water were soothing. He was unsure what he was looking for, but the mountain held a secret, and he wanted to uncover it. The boat came to a halt, and he stepped on to solid ground.

Tall trees almost seem to touch the sky. The small team of men began hiking to the spot, which matched Daisy's pictures. After three hours of trekking, they reached the location. The ground was solid, and the grass untouched. The team searched the entire area for three hours and found nothing. They also dug holes to uncover hidden doors, but the mountain refused to reveal its secrets.

In the late afternoon, he called off the search, and the disappointed men headed home. Their quest had yielded nothing. Once the boats reached the other end of the swamp, his men began unloading the equipment. Norris stood with his arms crossed.

Maybe it was some other mountain, he thought, *maybe it was just a hoax.*

County Morgue

William had his own challenges for the day. The unidentified objects and the graphs presented a mystery he was afraid he couldn't solve. Focusing on the graphs, he could barely see the date, but when he placed them next to each other, he noticed a pattern. Whatever the graphs were measuring was increasing. The x and y-axis on the graphs were not clear because the document hadn't been scanned properly or was very old.

"Definitely a result of something. Maybe a lab report. Of what? What were they testing?"

He didn't know. It made little sense. But one thing was sure, this could have been a motive to kill Lauren.

His phone rang, and it was Tom.

"Afternoon, detective," William said.

"Hey…"

Tom looked better today and sat in his small, comfortable office. "Hey… how are you?" he said.

"I'm well. You?" William asked.

"Can't complain."

"Tell me, have you found out anything more about Lauren?" William inquired.

"Yep. I spoke with the editor and got a list of articles that she was working on. I tried to get to her apartment, but after a month of her disappearance, the landlord sent her stuff over to the parents and found a new lodger."

"Not uncommon."

"I have called the parents and I am heading off to see them."

"Sounds good."

"She was working with two environmentalists, trying to understand how the planet was changing. But from what I gather, she had nothing substantial. Nothing specific about the swamp."

"Then why did she come here?"

"Well, her boss said he didn't authorize it."

"Really?"

"Yes."

The men fell silent.

Tom stood up, grabbed his badge, pulled on his winter jacket, armed himself, and then covered his face with a mask. He looked as if he was headed into a battlefield.

"I am heading off now. I'll talk to you later."

William simply nodded.

Before he could focus again, the phone rang.

"Hello Dr. Sterling, this is Usher here."

"Hey how is it going?"

"Good… good. You always seem to find something for me to do."

William laughed.

Usher Downing worked in the New York Department

of Public Health. He was an expert in detecting toxins in soil and water and worked with several environmentalists. However, his department was currently focused on identifying the spread of COVID-19 in the water system. William felt he might have pulled Usher away from a very important task, but he needed answers.

"I got your samples from the crime scene."

"Oh, it wasn't at the crime scene."

"Oh, I see,"

"Okay… What did you find?"

"The water contains a high level of mercury. It is poisonous to humans and any life form in the water body."

William held his head. Several men, including himself, had entered the swamp during the search.

"Dr. Sterling, if it wasn't from the crime scene, where did you get the sample from?"

"A swamp in Nightridge."

Usher hesitated. "Is there a chemical factory around the village?"

"No, not that I know of. Is it likely to spread to the open sea?"

"Yes, if its source is not found quickly… it will!"

William became silent.

"Dr. Sterling, I have to report this to the authorities."

"Yes. Yes. I understand."

"It might undermine your investigation, but no one… no one should enter that swamp, is that clear?"

"Yes, of course."

"You should warn the mayor and the sheriff."

William nodded absentmindedly.

"Okay. I will stay in touch."

The call ended, and William sat back.

Maybe that's why Lauren was here, he thought. He straightened and turned to the graphs in front of him.

"These could be mercury levels," he muttered.

Sheriff's Office

The smoke from the cigar flew out of the window as Norris reread his notes on the case. He had received a call from William about the mercury in the swamp. It was agitating, but not unbelievable. He asked Mrs. Flores to contact the nearest Public Health department and arrange for testing. He also asked her to draft a memorandum to circulate in the village, to let everyone know that the swamp was off-limits. All men who had entered the swamp had to get tested. He blew the smoke out of his mouth. It seemed to calm him down.

He focused back on the case. He picked up the phone and called the local doctor.

"Good evening, Chief."

"Good evening, Dr. Hendrik. How are you doing this evening?"

"I am well. I am well. Thank you. What about you?"

"I am puzzled."

"Huh... how can I help?"

"Can you tell me if Daisy was in good health?"

"Hmm... let me see. Well, except for some anemia, she was fine. I prescribed her some medicine for that. But her mother told me she never took them."

"Ah. I see. Anything else?"

"No."

"Did she behave oddly?"

"Well, no. Like every teenager, she didn't like to be told what to do and hated medical checkups."

Norris smiled. That was typical.

Local Hospital

Darkness fell, and the town was soundless. Norris wanted to see Nicholas and entered the hospital late afternoon. The doctors had told him that Nicholas would be discharged soon. Norris knew it was a bad idea, he needed time. Grief of losing a family is exponential and Nicholas would have to face it one day, just like Norris had to face losing a part of his family.

He knocked twice, opened the door, and found Nicholas standing, staring out of the window as if lost in an oblivion.

"Nicholas," Norris said.

No response.

"Nicholas?" he called again, stepping forward.

A pair of red, swollen eyes glared at him. His face was as pale as a ghost. He had certainly lost weight and looked balder. Norris wondered if the doctors were actually looking after him.

"Are you feeling, okay?"

Nicholas hung his head and slowly sat on the chair. He scratched the bandages on his left hand.

"How are you feeling?"

"Like a man who has lost everything."

County Morgue

Wearing gloves, William reached for the cabinet below the bench and took out the containers. He had hidden them from Fredrick. He thought it was best not to tell him. The three objects remained still. Placing it under a magnifying glass, he observed the one he had cut open. Biting his lips, he zoomed in. It was the same. He saw a panel with circuits and black square surfaces. It frightened him, not knowing what it was. Carefully putting it on a slide, and then on the stage of the microscope, he turned on the illumination. He sat in awe for a moment and stepped away. He meticulously placed the first object aside and then reached for the second one. With shaking hands, he cautiously sliced open the second one. To the naked eye, it appeared the same. He picked up the magnifying glass and observed.

It looks identical; he thought.

He mounted it on a slide and observed it under the microscope. There wasn't much difference in both objects. He labeled it and placed it beside the first one.

As soon as he mounted the third one, he knew it was different. Along with the circuits, it had an empty tube. It could be to hold something. He bit his lip and put it aside.

Oh, Jack, I wish you were here, he thought

He placed specimen A under the microscope, adjusted the magnification, and grabbed the high-definition camera. Placing the camera on the eyepiece of the micro-scope, he adjusted the zoom and clicked.

It took him about half an hour to get several shots of all the specimens. Then he transferred the images to the

PC and emailed Jack. With a heavy heart, he took the phone and called him.

After explaining to Jack what he had found, William hung up the phone. As expected, Jack was dumbfounded and angry he hadn't told him before.

Norris parked his truck in front of the mortuary's door, and as expected, the lights were on. Dr. Sterling never left on time. Most of his deputies were home, watching television with their families and discussing their adventures. This man from the city was hard on facts, and the time of the day did not matter to him. Norris opened the door, anticipating the doctor to be doing paperwork. Instead, he found him staring at printouts. Stepping closer, he found William observing what looked like circuit boards.

William's phone rang, and Norris pushed the green button.

A young man's face popped up on the screen.

"Hello," Norris said to the young man on the screen.

"Hey," he replied.

"Jack, meet Sheriff Cunningham. Sheriff, this is Jack," William said.

Norris nodded.

Jack smiled, "Nice to meet you."

William explained to Norris that Jack was helping them with the case. Especially the mystery surrounding the spider and the anomaly.

"What spider?" asked Norris. "What anomaly?"

William straightened, as if realizing his oversight. "Sorry. Let's discuss the spider first. About the anomaly, I will let you know when I find out more."

Norris nodded.

"Dr. Sterling found the image of a spider in the USB drive," said Jack.

"Oh. Which one is it?"

"You don't want to be near this thing."

"It's deadly?" William asked.

"One of the deadliest spiders in the world. It's called Phoneutria. Its bite affects the nervous system and, if not treated, can kill you. Tell me these things are not native to Nightridge."

William looked at Norris.

"I have not seen one around here."

"Let's keep it that way, shall we?" remarked Jack.

"What else did you find?"

"Out of curiosity, I tried to find where these things are found except in their natural habitat. Can you believe people keep them as pets? Man, people are sick."

"I am sure some people in New York keep cockroaches as pets," said William.

Norris rolled his eyes. Surely he was joking.

"Yeah, right! These people have nothing better to do. Spiders... of all things. There are no hard and fast regulations against keeping such spiders. But there should be!"

"Get to the point, Jack," William said.

"I started asking around or looking for people who sold or collected these ugly things. There are only a handful of people who keep these. Guess what? Mr. Henry Rogers, the mayor of Nightridge, is also a collector."

A chill ran down Norris's spine.

"Are you sure?"

"I am damn sure. He bought it as a pet six months

ago. I don't know why he bought it, and I think that is a very dangerous and ugly pet."

Meadow Cottage

William was drained, physically and mentally. He saw Norris was tired as well. While Norris was in the shower, he stepped into the kitchen and made sure the fish was well cooked. "Ah... thank you," said Norris as he dried his hair with a towel.

"Least I could do. I feel like I am taking over your home."

"I don't mind you staying here. There is only one motel in this village, and it closed down. No thanks to the pandemic."

"Yes. It has changed many things."

"Including relationships?" commented Norris, and grabbed two beers from the fridge. "Tell me you are not living all alone in that big bad city."

William laughed. "No. Not really."

Norris raised his eyebrows, "But you wish you were."

"Yes. I wished I had known what I was getting into."

"Ah. It will sort itself out. Don't worry."

William wasn't sure.

They enjoyed the food with some salad. William noted Norris didn't even touch the salad. He guessed; Norris preferred meat. Living with Joan, he had gotten used to eating veggies.

After they finished dinner, Norris said, "I need your opinion."

William wiped his mouth with a tissue. "On what?"

Norris got up, walked to the table, and returned with a folder. "We took several photos of the mountain. There is nothing up there, but I can't help thinking I missed something."

"You want me to have a look?"

"I know you are busy, but I could use your insight."

"Sure!" William said, putting his fork down eagerly.

Norris remained patient as William flipped through the pictures.

"You have been to this spot on the mountain?"

"Yep."

William said nothing more and began comparing the photos of the mountain taken by Daisy and Norris.

Norris finished washing the dishes and put the leftovers in the fridge. William was still studying the pictures.

"This is something…" muttered William.

Norris came to stand beside him. In front of William were two pictures of the same spot. In one, it appeared as if something was emerging from the mountain. However, in the other picture, the terrain was flat.

"I have been to that spot, there is nothing there," Norris said.

"No. Look at the time stamp. Yours is 12.30 pm, and this is 1:00 am."

Norris straightened, and his eyes turned to the clock. It was nearing 10:00 pm.

27

FINDING SATAN

16th February 2020 (Present day)
Bridge

Norris grabbed the bar, and his feet hung in midair.

"Chief, are you okay?" Kyle yelled.

Norris gathered his strength and pushed himself upwards. His heart was beating so fast, he thought he would have a heart attack. Ignoring his fears, he pushed himself upwards, and within minutes, was standing on the crossbars of the walkway. He couldn't believe his luck; he might have died.

"Chief, are you okay?" yelled Kyle again.

"Yeah!" he shouted back.

He took a few minutes to catch his breath and find his courage. Grabbing the rods tightly, he took one step after another. The water rushed under him, and mist blew with the wind clouding his vision.

"One step at a time," he said, "one step at a time."

His hands turned icy. It felt like ages, but he finally reached the other end. Making sure he wouldn't lose his balance, he eyed the bridge's pillar. It divided into several spokes, which vanished into the vast structure. Taking a deep breath, he reached for his bag and grabbed a bomb, placing it in a spoke of the bridge. He turned on the timer, which was set to thirty minutes.

He felt a sense of accomplishment, but his work wasn't done. The walkway shook, and he grabbed the handles. It was old, rusty, and swayed with the wind. The mist was becoming thicker. He overheard the bells of the town hall.

Cautiously, he returned to the other side and placed the second bomb. Once he was sure he had positioned the explosive correctly, he found his way back to the circular platform along the pillar. Hugging the cement pillar, he plodded toward the iron ladder. He had almost made it. Suddenly, he realized the surface of the pillar was flat, and he had nothing to grab on as a support. He couldn't sway; he would have to jump.

"I am too old for this," he muttered.

"Chief, hold on. I am coming," called out Kyle.

But they had no time. The bridge had to be destroyed. He took in a deep breath, gathered all his courage, and leaped.

Nightridge

William tried to remain calm as he glared into the reverend Benson's eyes. He felt the edge of the knife on his neck. The reverend's breath was foul, sweat covered his face, and murder filled his eyes.

"Are you Satan?" asked the reverend in a horrid voice.

"No," William replied. He waved his hand, signaling Tom and the others to stay back. Benson clasped his neck, and his eyes bore into his soul.

"You wouldn't lie to me, would you?" said Benson.

Swallowing hard, William said, "No."

The reverend looked around suspiciously, but his grip remained around William's neck.

"He is out here... somewhere... he started this. He is to blame. If I kill him, everything will go back to normal. No more screams. No more shouts. No more pandemic... peace would return. I'll find Satan."

William remained silent.

Pointing the knife close to William's eyes, he said, "You wouldn't lie to me, would you?"

"No. I won't."

"I know you saw him. Tell me, where did he go?"

William said nothing.

"Tell me!"

William remembered Jack had told him that a group of villagers were heading north.

"Which way?" growled the priest.

He pointed south. "That way. He went that way."

Growling, he looked down the street. "We are all conduits. We are all connected.... He started this.... I will finish it!" he said. "And then you will be free. We all will be free." He pushed William to the ground.

Screaming at the top of his lungs, the priest ran down the street, vanishing into the thick fog.

William shook with fear.

"Are you nuts? He could have killed you!" Tom cried out, coming to his side. "You should have knocked him out."

William quickly got up and touched his neck. Blood smeared his fingers. "I have done a lot of bad things in my life; I didn't want to add punching a priest to the list."

Tom rolled his eyes.

28

MOUNTAIN OF SECRETS

11th February 2020
The Swamp

I t was a crazy idea, but they were rowing the boat toward the mountain. It was dead silent, aside from the mosquitoes buzzing around Norris's head as he tried to stay focused on paddling.

His day had been confusing and appalling. He wanted to confront Henry about the spider, but the mayor wasn't at home, nor was his wife. That was rather unusual.

They reached the mountain and began their trek in the dark. Norris checked his gun. He knew, due to William's short training in the Navy, he could defend himself, but nothing human lived in these parts.

They followed their previous trail and trekked until they came to the edge of the mountain. They admired the open sea to one side, and the swamp was just behind them. The ground shook, and Norris grabbed the tree next to him. They exchanged worried glances. Again, the ground trembled, and a loud crack emitted from ahead of them.

"Let's go!" William yelled.

Norris ran toward the noise, and William followed him. As they came to a clearing, they saw a bright light emerging from the ground. Norris couldn't believe his eyes. The doorway remained open for a while and then began to close.

"Come on," William said, rushing in the direction of the closing doors.

"No! Wait!"

But it was too late. William jumped in first, followed by Norris.

Cold steel hit Norris's face. Breathless, he sat up, rubbing his arm. William had fallen on the steps and was cradling his knee.

"Ah…" William cried out.

"You, okay?" Norris asked.

William nodded. "It will settle. Give me a minute."

Forgetting his pain or breathlessness, Norris watched his surroundings in amazement. He grabbed the railing and slowly stood up, unable to believe it. They were in an underground cavern with rows of tube lights. He turned to his left and caught sight of a few big rectangular boxes almost the size of his refrigerator. Several lights danced on the surface of the boxes.

"It's a server," said William. "I have seen them at Cranston Enterprises."

"What is it doing here?"

"You tell me."

Norris had no answer. He felt as if he had landed on an alien planet.

They slowly came down the stairs and looked at the fine tiles covered in brown dust. The roof was made up of bare mountain. Rocks, lumps of soil, and roots were visible. The air-conditioner was on, and it was too cold. Four tall and broad cylinders, rounded at the top, stood in a corner.

Norris moved forward and saw a long table with coffee mugs on top catching dust. Several blank screens remained in place and a couple of CPUs were on the floor. As he neared, he caught a whiff of a peculiar smell

"Oh my god," cried William.

Norris turned and gasped. In a large glass box were several Phoneutria spiders.

"What are they doing here?"

"I do not know."

"Let's not touch that!"

Norris nodded. "What is this place?"

"Looks like a secret... abandoned lab."

Norris agreed. "But then why did the doors open?"

William shrugged his shoulders and walked to the table. On a hunch, he stepped forward and pushed a key. All the monitors came to life, displaying blue screens with a design in the corner. Norris observed the three-drop logo. A pop-up box appeared, asking for a password.

"Passwords? That is not my area. We'll need help," William said, grabbing his phone, then brooded. "What happened?" Norris asked.

"No signal. What about yours?"

Norris checked his mobile and shook his head. William took photos of the computers and the server.

"Who opened the door?" Norris asked, studying the deserted place.

"I think it was the computer," William replied. "Maybe it has been programmed to open the door at a certain time."

"Why?"

"Beats me," William answered, turning toward tall cylinders. "They are cold," he remarked, touching them.

"If we want answers, we need to get into the computers," said Norris.

"Hm... I wonder," William said, and sat in front of a computer.

"What are you doing?"

William typed. All the screens came to life.

"What? How did you know the password?"

He turned. "I just typed in the spider's name."

Norris nodded appreciatively. Several questions ran through his head. What was this place? Who built it and when? He waited for an answer as William searched the computer.

William sighed. "They have wiped out everything."

"What? Are you sure?"

"Yes. Someone cleared the hard drive. I can't get anything."

"Can your tech friend help us?"

"We can try," William replied.

Marching to the entrance, he went up the stairs,

looking for a signal. "Yes!" he said and quickly sent the message.

Norris walked toward the cylinders, and William joined him. As they walked around one of them, they found a small panel with a green blinking button. Before he think of all possibilities, William pushed the button.

"No…" Norris said, but it was too late.

The cylinder vibrated, and its steel exterior turned, and a glass tank full of green liquid became visible. For a second, Norris thought he saw a shadow. The bubbling liquid moved upwards, and within the green glow, he saw a face.

"Ah," William gasped.

They moved back. A skull with its mouth open and hollow eyes stared at them. As they waited, the rest of the body became clear, or whatever was left of it. The bones had turned brown and looked as if they were melting.

"What the hell is going on here?" William asked.

Norris didn't know. The man must have died months ago, but why keep him suspended like this? Why not bury or burn him? Norris didn't have any answers. He noticed a small stool and shoes and an apron lying near the tank. Did someone throw him in there? Or did he decide to end his life?

William found a small ladder and put it against the cylinder. He climbed up.

"What can you see?" Norris called out.

"A hatch."

"Okay, anyone could have put him in there."

William's face turned pale.

"What?"

"I don't think this was murder."

"Suicide?"

"Yes."

"There are no marks on the tank. A murderer wouldn't bother removing his victims' shoes or apron. Also, if someone pushed him in there, the body would have been upside down. No. He jumped."

Norris held his head. Four people were dead.

William came down the ladder.

"Can we get him out?"

"I don't think so. We need to get some answers before we get him out of there."

Norris agreed and then turned his attention toward the next cylinder. They glanced at each other.

"I hope not," William said.

"Me too…"

With a heavy heart, he pushed the button. The cylinder didn't vibrate. This was also full of green liquid. They waited. Norris relaxed his shoulders as he realized that there was no corpse in this one.

A whooshing noise filled the area. William had opened the last two cylinders. He walked close to look at the green bubbling liquid and waited.

"Nobody," said William.

"Well, that's good."

They stood wondering. They had found another body, spiders, and had more questions than answers. As they neared the exit, Norris eyed the door.

"We are trapped!"

William cleared his throat and pushed a red button on the wall. The doors opened.

As they emerged from the hidden lab, it was still dark. Norris asked William not to tell anyone about the place until they had more answers. William agreed. The truth was, Norris didn't know who built this lab or why? Several questions crowded his mind, and he wondered if he would ever find the answers.

29

PUSHING LIMITS

16th February 2020 (Present day)
Bridge

Norris knew this was a bad idea. He leaped, his hand reaching for the ladder. Suddenly, he slipped. He cried out but luckily grabbed a rod. A sharp pain ran through his arm as he quickly found his footing. His entire life rushed before his eyes. He knew he was pushing his limits. Would tonight be the end? Would he join his wife, son, and grandson? He closed his eyes and rested his head against the ladder.

"Chief! Chief!"

He heard a loud engine and saw a bright light on the highway.

"Someone's coming!" Kyle exclaimed.

With no time to waste, Norris came down the ladder. He ran along the river bank and found Kyle waiting for him. Norris checked the time. The bomb would blow in five minutes. The sound of the raging river drowned the engine's noise. A pair of headlights approached towards the bridge.

The blast was deafening. The bridge blew and pieces flew in every direction. A large ball of fire raged toward the sky, followed by an enormous cloud of black smoke. The bridge crumbled. When Norris looked up, only the two ends of the bridge remained. He was happy and terrified. The zombies couldn't leave town, but nor could they.

Nightridge

William halted when he heard a scream. The group behind him paused. In the silence and the darkness, they shuddered in fear. Tom remained alert, Fredrick looked up and down nervously, and the children, to William's surprise, remained quiet.

William rushed down the street, and the others followed. Most of the houses were on fire. The mob had trashed the other homes. Doors were open. Gardens destroyed. Garbage littered the road, and the foul smell of rubbish and urine filled the air.

He paused. They were halfway there, and there was no sign of anyone. Although Jack had told him the coast was clear, he kept his guard up. Either they were very lucky or they were being watched.

"Keep going," Tom whispered.

William nodded. The streetlights were dim, and the darkness bothered him. They jogged toward the house that was just around the corner.

William looked behind. The children were trying to keep up, but their little feet were not quick enough. Tom was at the end; he was leading the group, and Fredrick remained in the middle.

They came up to a street, and William froze. Three figures walked toward them.

"Shit… shit…" he whispered, motioning the group to hide. He grabbed one girl and lifted her over the fence. The others did the same. Once the kids were on the other side, the adults hopped over.

"Move… now… hide…" Tom whispered.

They hid behind a thick row of rosemary, sitting quietly, close together. He glanced at the children. The younger ones remained with the teacher, and the older ones huddled together in groups. William watched through the gap between the leaves and saw Billy. His face was pasty white, and his eyes remained open as if in a trance.

Oh no, not this guy, he thought.

Billy groaned and clattered his teeth. William eyed the axes each of them carried. They were still dripping with blood. His heart sank. A part of him wanted to shoot them down but backed off. The terrified little faces looked at him with hope. They needed William more.

The footsteps quietened, and William slowly peeped over the rosemary. He told the others to stay hidden. William cautiously stepped out and looked up and down the street. The coast was clear.

"Let's go!" he whispered.

The group moved. William helped the kids over the fence. Together, they hurried toward the dark two-story house. William took out the keys from his pocket, unlocked the door, and everyone rushed in. He closed the door behind them and locked it. The children whimpered.

"Shush... shush," said Ms. Pritchard.

"I want my mommy."

She picked up the little girl and hugged her.

"Soon, soon. It will all be over. I promise it will be okay. We are safe now. We are safe," she said, eying William.

William entered the study and saw the computer and the server. The server looked identical to the one in the lab. They were back in the game.

"Fredrick, get to work."

Fredrick moved hastily and turned on the laptop.

"Liaise with Jack and link the computer with the server."

Fredrick nodded and started working. William grabbed a charger and connected his phone.

"It's done... connected. I have this computer linked with the laptop," Fredrick said.

"Uplink the server so that Jack can control it remotely."

"Agreed," said Fredrick.

William looked at the group.

"Stay here," he told Fredrick.

"Come on," William said, leading the group down the corridor. Once they entered the basement, everyone gasped. William studied the shock on the teacher's face. Henry and Hector sat in a corner, tied down, and gagged.

"What's this?" Ms. Pritchard said, horrified, "What the hell is this?"

"No matter what, do not untie them. Do you understand? Yours and the children's lives depend on it." He grabbed her shoulders. "Do you understand!"

Terror filled her eyes. A sudden loud bang and a horrid scream startled them. The children cried out, sprinting to a corner.

"And don't open that door!" Tom added.

30

IMAGES

12th February 2020
Meadow Cottage

Their trip up the mountain was tiresome. As they entered the house, William eyes began to shut. He changed into his pajamas and fell asleep instantly.

A loud sound awakened him. William rubbed his eyes and he glanced at the clock. It was midday.

"Oh, damn."

A quick shower woke him up, and he rushed downstairs, buttoning his shirt. He found Norris drinking coffee, looking out of the window.

"Afternoon," William said

"Afternoon." Norris replied.

They spoke very little and then both left for work.

County Morgue

William returned to the morgue, ready for work. He placed his mobile on the table, expecting a call from Juliet and perhaps Roumoult. William had sent all the information about the secret lab to Jack and was waiting for a response.

Since he was still waiting for Daisy's results, he focused his attention on Lauren. The slides were ready, and he began looking at them one by one.

At the end of three hours, he concluded her blood was clean. No toxin, no drugs, no alcohol. He didn't see the need to examine her brain. The cause of death was the gunshot wound. Satisfied with his work, he closed the file and put it aside.

His phone rang, and Juliet Wave's face appeared on the screen. He had been waiting for the Forensic Pathologist's call. William noticed that Juliet's features had pallid, and she had lost weight. Her blonde hair was tied up in a messy bun, and a pair of glasses sat on her long, thin nose. She looked tired, and her eyes were swollen.

"Hey!"

"Hi," she said.

"How are you?"

"Surviving," she replied gravely, "Our neighbor died yesterday."

William's heart sunk. Juliet had known Mrs. Mason for twenty years, and they were good friends. The pandemic was hard on everyone, especially the old and fragile.

"I am so sorry."

"You know, she didn't even have a funeral. She died alone." Juliet paused and sobbed.

"I am so sorry."

He waited for her to calm down.

"We need to do something," she said in a low voice.

"We are doing all we can. You know that. Everyone is trying their best," he said, knowing he was lying. They could do more.

It took a while for Juliet to settle down. "Since I couldn't sleep much last night, I did the tests," she said.

"Okay. Did you find anything?" William said, glad to change the subject. He didn't want his friend to cry.

"The brain samples you sent show traces of a neurotoxin. I found inflammation, necrosis, and congestion."

"Could the neurotoxin be the reason for her inappropriate behavior?"

"Not likely. But it killed her."

"The toxin could have induced the heart failure?"

"Yes. My hypothesis is the neurotoxin entered her system and took over quickly. First, it affected the neurons, causing acute apoptosis and hemorrhage. The heart tried to compensate, but eventually, when the toxin reached the heart, it triggered fatal arrhythmia leading to sudden cardiac arrest."

"What was the toxin?"

"Looks like venom."

William looked at her. "Spider venom?"

"Or snake…"

William stood up and started pacing. "Any ideas on how it entered her body?"

"Bite," Juliet said, stating the obvious.

"No. I checked. There were no signs of a snake or spider bites on her body," William answered, but then recalled the minor wound on Daisy's leg. Maybe she was stung by a spider. If that was the case, she would have needed medical attention immediately.

"I have gone through all your notes, and I have completed all the tests. I haven't found evidence of anything except the neurotoxin."

"But..."

"There was a high level of serotonin and dopamine."

William raised his eyebrows. "Okay..."

"But the most interesting thing is the high level of the neurotransmitter glutamate."

"Glutamate..."

"Yep. In a normal brain, it is present in over ninety percent of the brain synapses and signals other cells in the brain. It's a controller of the brain, and its levels must be tightly regulated. It helps us form memories and also tells the brain what to do."

William nodded.

"It is an excitatory neurotransmitter, and Daisy's brain was flooded with it."

"She wasn't thinking right."

"Yes. And with the mixture of dopamine and serotonin, she would have lost all control. The slightest thing would have provoked her."

"She didn't have any history of mental illness. What about drug use?"

"She's clean... no drugs."

They fell silent.

"It has to be something that stimulated the hippocampus..."

"It might have affected the amygdala..."

"Agreed, hippocampus stimulation increases the levels

of neurotransmitters. Maybe the first thing it affected was the amygdala, the main center of the brain that controls all human emotions, including fear and rage."

William started getting worried. He thought about the anomalies he had found. Did they change her brain chemistry? Was it a new contagion? He wished Jack would come back to him with more answers.

Unaware of his thoughts, Juliet continued, "Such a person would lose all sense of reality and become very violent."

"And kill?"

"In a nutshell, Daisy, she would have killed that morning or the next day."

William leaned on the table.

"I also spoke to a neurologist. He says a person with unregulated neurotransmitters could become violent, full of rage and will lose all touch with reality."

"How long would it last?"

"I don't know. From your notes, Daisy killed her mother, attacked her father, and then died within, say, five minutes. That means whatever this is, it's very potent. So far, we have only one victim. Maybe other people were exposed too. If yes, how do we find them before they become violent and kill?"

Sheriff's Office

Norris dropped by the hospital. Nicholas looked well today. His face was better, and the nurses reported that he had eaten well. He still looked tired, but hearing that he had made some progress pleased him.

Then Norris headed to his office and checked old construction records. A lab that big had to be created by someone, and it would require labor.

He went through years of records and found nothing that accounted for any kind of construction. He became disappointed. After going through his case notes, he remembered something. He dialed William's number.

"Yes," the doctor said.

"Have you got the list of the articles Lauren was working on?"

"Yes."

"Please send them to me."

Half an hour passed, and Norris got immersed in administrative work. Mrs. Flores waited for him to finish. Daisy's case had been a massive distraction, and he had no time to do his regular tasks. His computer beeped, and an email from William came through. With high anticipation, he opened it and there it was: the list of articles.

31

LOST CONNECTIONS

16th February 2020 (Present day)
Bridge

Looking at the shattered bridge, Norris felt sorrow. He wondered if they would ever rebuild it. A roar of an engine drove him out of his thoughts. He signed toward Kyle and stepped back under cover. They waited, and the car came to a stop. A man and a woman stepped out. The woman screamed.

"We have to get out… we have to get out! I have to leave! Leave this stinky place!"

The man walked to the edge.

"Oh, no…" mumbled Norris.

"This is your doing! It's all your fault! You dragged me here! You will be the death of me!" shouted the man.

"What do we do?" Kyle asked.

They hadn't expected this. The villagers weren't rational. They could jump, attempt to swim, or think they could fly. What had they done?

The man screamed and kicked the car. He yelled at the woman. The woman picked up a rock and threw it at him. The man fell to the ground.

"Go to hell!" she yelled and got behind the wheel.

"What should we do?" asked Kyle.

"If they choose to jump off the bridge or shoot each other, there is nothing we can do. All we can do is pray."

The car started, the headlights moved away from the bridge, and then vanished. Norris let out a sigh of relief.

Nightridge

William sat in silence, and he was sure he had freaked out Ms. Pritchard and the kids. But they had no choice. They didn't trust Henry or Hector. They could complicate the situation. Glancing at the woman and the children, William left.

Back in the study, he and Tom pulled down the shades. In the dark, they worked in silence. The graphs on the screens hadn't changed. The nanobots were active. It was time to disable them.

"How is it going?" William inquired.

"We are linking the computer to the server. It will take time," Fredrick said.

Tom and William exchanged glances.

"We need to get the truck. Jack, is it safe?"

They focused on a monitor which showed the bird's-eye view of the village. Several dots lined the screen.

"Where is it?"

"Near the timber mill…"

Jack zoomed in, and they saw the mayor's house and

the mill. There were a couple of specks scattered over the area. They could sneak through.

"Let's go."

William wished there was a better way. The jog back to the truck was tougher than he thought. Either he was fatigued or scared. Once they had left the house, he messaged Jack, who had told him that their path was clear. But still William felt as if someone was watching them.

Breathless, they reached the mill and entered the structure. William was pleased to see the truck.

"I don't believe Roumoult gave the drones to you."

"Well… he made me promise a few things."

They walked toward the vehicle.

"Really what?"

"First, I would get to Nightridge one way or another."

"Okay," William said.

"And I would bring you back."

William was happy. "Sounds like him."

"Oh… yeah… and before I forget," Tom said. He stepped forward and punched him in the face. William stumbled backwards.

"What the hell was that for?" he demanded, touching his jaw.

"He told me to punch you in the face for keeping him in the dark!"

William eyed him. "You enjoyed that, didn't you?"

"Yep!"

When Tom turned the key, the truck made a loud noise. William was scared it would attract attention. He told Tom to drive as fast as possible, but it was a small truck carrying a heavy load. William messaged Jack to alert them if any of the villagers were nearby.

He let out a sigh of relief when they reached the house, and Tom reversed the truck into the enormous garage. By the time they parked the truck, the garage door closed.

William jumped out of the truck. He could still feel his jaw ache. But couldn't argue with Tom, and Roumoult was right. William should have told them sooner. Maybe they could have called for help sooner.

In the study, they found Fredrick on a video call with Jack and Roumoult. They looked concerned. Roumoult walked up and down in a dimly lit room with the phone against his ear.

"Okay," Fredrick said. "the connection to the server is complete. We must get the drones ready."

"But before that, we need to activate the booster," Jack mentioned.

William and Tom looked at each other.

32

THE PLANET SAVER

12th February 2020
Sheriff's Office

The sun had almost vanished behind the trees, and his staff had left long ago. But Norris kept reading the articles. Most of them covered political agendas and how they had led to the destruction of forests and the changes in the environment. Power was something all governments craved, and they were exhausting the earth's natural resources that would lead to complicating all life on our planet. Norris agreed.

Then there were articles about the unseen war or coronavirus, and Lauren spent days studying the pattern of the spread of the pandemic. Her articles were thought provoking, and he could see the hate and love she got on the web after publishing her work. But it didn't seem to deter the journalist.

The next few articles were about an iconic figure. Mr. Bryan Sanders. Norris had heard of him. A philanthropist with a vision of the new world. Norris didn't like people who wanted to design the world according to their view. But the world didn't run on his will either.

He gathered from the articles that several 'indications' of Mr. Sanders developing breakthrough technology would turn the tables. There was constant mention of a technique to improve control over the human mind.

A chill ran down his spine.

The research tool was designed to be used in patients with neurological diseases. They claimed they could improve the physiological function in patients with disabilities caused by an impaired brain or brain damage. It was dangerous; it was unethical, and yet it was one of the prime directives of his organization. Lauren was clearly not his fan, and her articles urged her readers to think about how this technology could affect humanity's future.

Norris turned to his computer and read more. Lauren was not alone. Thousands of people online were protesting this research, which brought considerable negative media attention to the company.

The media had brought the research project to the attention of big organizations like the UN and FDA, who considered it unethical and were obviously not on his side. Mr. Sanders had been ordered to shut down the project about six months ago. There was no evidence that he had actually shut the project down, but his research company went bankrupt. After the order from the FDA, the public seemed to move on and then everyone had other things to worry about, like the coronavirus.

He backtracked the blogs, articles until the end of 2018 and found that Lauren was one of the first investigative journalists to publish a controversial article about this technology.

That is the motive for murder, he thought.

His phone rang, and he answered it without thinking. It was Detective Tom Nash.

"Hello old friend, how are you doing?" asked Tom.

"I am well, thanks. How are you?"

"Good. Surviving."

"I guess William has updated you about the case."

"Yes. And I had some information that he asked me to tell you directly."

"Oh?"

"It's about Lauren. I went to see her parents, who were devastated to find out that we found their daughter in a swamp."

Norris became silent.

"I got access to her personal belongings that were sent by her landlord to the parents. Nothing out of the ordinary, except her laptop. With the parents' permission, I took the laptop into my possession and handed it over to the tech department at the NYPD."

"Did they find anything?"

"Yes. The reason Lauren went to Nightridge. Check your email."

Norris did as he was told. He saw pictures of several unidentified men on two boats in the swamp, loaded with white cylinders.

"The cylinders?"

"Yes. According to Lauren, the white cylinders might have contained toxic residues from a chemical plant about thirty miles south of the village. Her sources informed her it could be mercury."

"How did she know?"

"Her notes say that an unidentified source sent her the pictures of the illegal dump. She probably went there to investigate if it was true before she published anything."

Norris held his head, "They could have killed her for that."

"Yes."

"Or while she was gathering evidence, she noticed the lab in the mountain."

"The what?" asked Tom.

Norris explained to the detective what they had found.

"Oh, that explains why William is rattled."

"So, there are two parties who had a lot to lose if Lauren continued her work."

"Yes. I am going to say something you will not like. It could be someone in the village."

Their eyes met.

"No!"

"Lauren was dedicated to the planet. From what I gather, she cared very little about herself, loved nature, and would have done anything to save it. Norris, people were listening to her, following her. She was becoming a leader. She was becoming a threat."

Norris didn't like it, but it could be true.

"The murderer might be closer to home than you think."

County Morgue

William had sent pictures of the unidentified object to Jack. He hadn't heard from him for over 48 hours. He was thinking of calling him when he received a call.

"Hey..." Jack said in a low voice.

"It's good to see you," William said, trying to be cheerful.

"When I asked you to send me something exciting, I never thought it would be this," he said, sharing an image William had sent.

"What is it?"

"Well, in short, a robot."

William was petrified. He sat down on the stool.

"What do you mean?"

"A really tiny robot."

William looked at the containers. "Is it alive?"

"No. I don't think so. It either ran out of power or has been damaged. I need to be there to see it."

"No. You can't come here."

"Fine. Well, it looks like a nanoprobe or nanobot."

"What the hell is that?"

"Nano means... small, and probe means something that is designed for diagnostic purposes."

"Like?"

"Biotechnology is advancing. In the medical world, nanoprobes are used to identify cancer cells. They act like indicators of diseased cells, which is useful for doctors and scientists. For now, these have a limited and non-lethal function."

"What about nanobots?"

"Nanobots are robots that in the near future will be used to deliver medicine. Mostly, all diseases are treated with pills or capsules, and those pass through the digestive system. Unfortunately, these drugs not only lose potency but cause a lot of side effects. However, if a nanobot carries the drug, it could use the circulatory system to reach the diseased affected area and release the drug locally for more effectiveness."

"That's interesting…"

"Yes, and I thought experimental… until today."

William turned to the containers.

"Well, nanobots or probes are used to gather data… to study… to deliver medicine…"

"To kill?" interposed William.

"Yes, it could be used to release a toxin or a poison at a certain time point when it reaches its destination."

William gulped. "Who could build this?"

Jack became thoughtful. "Have you heard of Sanders? He invested a lot in a technology that could control the brain. The scientist he was working with, Dr. Jason Walker, was a bio-technician… a genius and a pioneer in the field."

"Great, where can I find him?" William asked, getting excited.

"He has vanished without a trace."

William scrunched his forehead. "What do you mean?"

"About six months ago, Sanders gave up on the project and the lab closed down. No one saw Dr. Walker again."

"He's dead?"

"I don't know…"

"Can anyone else make this?"

"Well, I can design it, but if I do, the boss will cut me into small pieces and feed me to the wolves."

William rolled his eyes.

"You know, Roumoult is very sensitive about how technology could be misused. But he doesn't realize it's going to happen whether or not we like it. We can use any tool for good or bad. So, the question is, was this a tool or a murder weapon? And how many more did they make?"

Meadow Cottage

Norris sat staring at his empty plate. His conversation with Tom had got him thinking. He dropped by Henry's house and knocked on the door. There was no answer. He talked to his neighbors, and nobody had seen him. Then he inquired about Charlotte, the mayor's wife. It bothered him that the neighbors hadn't seen her for over ten days. Henry had told them she had stomach flu and was resting. But since then, no one had laid eyes on her.

The door opened, and a very concerned William entered the house.

"Hey," Norris said, trying to smile.

"Hi," William answered, and took a seat in front of him.

Norris gestured toward the stew, but William waved his hand.

"What's wrong?"

William looked him in the eye. "You will not like this."

"Funny, you are the second person to say that."

"Norris, there is a murderer out there who has access to technology that can enter a human undetected and could control their minds and urge them to do anything he or she wants."

Norris sat there, glaring at him, waiting for him to say that it was a joke. "What the hell are you talking about?"

"Daisy was injected with a nanobot. When activated, it altered or controlled her mind, and then it released a toxin that killed her."

"No. No. That is not possible!"

"It is. I am sorry. This is the most unbelievable but logical theory that explains her behavior and her death."

"But Lauren…"

"I think they killed Lauren because she came close to discovering something. Maybe she found the laboratory or the source of the illegal chemical dump. But I presume Daisy's death was a test. To see how this nanobot works."

Norris stood up. "You mean she could have been the first."

"Yes, and there could be more."

33

TWO SIDES OF A COIN

16th February 2020 (Present day)
Bridge

They were breathless by the time they reached the truck. Norris was happy to see it. Smoke dominated the western sky, and he thought they should tackle the fire. But right now, he had to focus on William's plan.

He jumped behind the wheel, and Kyle sat in the passenger seat. Norris glanced back. Mrs. Flores was still unconscious.

Please stay that way, he thought.

Norris felt dreadful, but he had little choice. He started the truck and swung the vehicle around. The ground was muddy, and he could feel the vehicle skid. He had to slow down, and that frustrated him. He reached for his gun with his left hand and checked the bullets. It was best to be prepared; they were going back into hell.

Nightridge

William and Tom sneaked into the garage and approached the container.

"How many drones have you got?" William asked.

"Around three hundred," Tom answered. "How are you going to control them?"

"There is a booster that links the drones with the computer and Jack will control them."

"You are remotely going to control these drones?" Tom said. "Okay. That sounds… less scary than dealing with zombies. What are these drones going to do?"

"They are going to target each villager and neutralize them."

"Neutralize?"

"Well, it's painful, but harmless. When the deputy stunned one of the zombies, the dot disappeared, and his link with the nanobot was severed."

Tom looked at him. "You intend to shock these people."

"It's better than killing them or watching them kill each other," argued William.

Tom gave it a thought. "Okay. You have three hundred drones, and there are about five thousand villagers. How are we going to do this?"

"We will load each with at least ten rounds of tasers."

"Not enough."

"We have no other choice. Roumoult is trying to get help… but it may not come."

William's phone buzzed. It was a text from Norris.

"The bridge has been destroyed."

William drew a deep breath in—one thing done. Now just one more thing to do. His eyes settled on the large gray container. Tom walked toward it and punched in the codes. It unlocked with a loud clang.

William helped pull the rack outwards. He saw hundreds of drones packed in bubble wraps, separated by layers of foam. Leaving the rack on a side, they walked in and dragged a box. It was the booster used to increase the signal of the drones.

"We have to carry this to the roof?" Tom asked unhappily, feeling its weight.

William nodded. "Yes. After we assemble it."

William didn't like it, but maybe it was for the best. He assigned Fredrick, Ms. Pritchard, and the children to assemble the drones. The children were opening the packing and handing it over to the adults who were putting it together. They placed the assembled drones back on the rack, ready to fly. Three children who were too young to understand sat in the corner, watching. They seem to be less edgy when they could see someone around them. While the others were busy with the drones, Tom and William assembled the booster.

After an hour, the hard work paid off. The booster was ready. It looked like a small bulky table with two antennae.

They carried the booster to the roof. William held the

hefty equipment as Tom secured its base by drilling in the screws.

Tom moved away, and William pushed a button. The box opened. At first, a thick rod appeared. It opened and resembled an upside-down umbrella. William reached for his mobile and called Jack.

"Okay, it's ready."

"You need to push the green button," said Jack.

William found the button underneath the booster and pushed it, but no sound came out. William looked at Tom. They jumped when they heard screams. They turned toward the burning village, and the fire had almost reached the forest. William's phone rang, and he heard the over-excited voice of Jack.

"We are good to go!"

34

AND THEN THERE WERE FIVE

13th February 2020
Local hospital

Norris and William entered the hospital. The nurse wasn't happy, but Norris didn't care. They entered Nicholas's room and found him standing, peering out of the window.

"Hi, Nicholas. We need to talk," said Norris and noticed William walked over and picked up Nicholas's medical charts.

Nicholas turned; his face paler than ever.

"Are you okay?" Norris asked.

He didn't reply. Norris noticed the bandages on his arms were smaller and his wounds appeared to be healing.

"Nicholas. We need to talk."

While still reading the files, William walked over to the door. Suddenly, he left the room.

Nicholas slowly sat down, folded his hands, and waited for him to speak.

Norris took a seat. "How are you?"

"Fine," he said in a hoarse voice.

"I am sorry. But I have to ask you something. Do you know Mr. Sanders?"

Nicholas raised his eyebrow. "I know him."

"How?"

"Had some dealing with him. Long time ago."

"What dealings?"

"He needed some construction material. I provided it."

"Where did you send it?"

"Send it? No. His men came and collected it."

"When was this?"

"About six years ago."

"Was Daisy involved in any way?"

Nicholas's face remained indifferent. "No."

"Did she know him?"

"No. I don't think so."

"Did he come to your home?"

"Yes. Six years ago, for dinner, but that was it."

William returned to the room and approached Norris.

"His serotonin levels are off the chart. I want to scan him," he stated in a low voice.

Norris turned to Nicholas and said, "Nicholas, you can help us understand what happened to Daisy."

Nicholas's eyes lit up. "Sure."

"We need to do a scan."

Nicholas looked puzzled.

William and Norris waited a while for Nicholas to get ready for the MRI scan. The technician appeared grumpy, but this time it wasn't a dead body. The scan began.

Images that made no sense to Norris flashed on the monitor.

"Focus on the head and neck," said William.

The technician nodded, and the pictures of bones, muscles in black and white appeared. It was like looking into space, just inside one's self.

"Stop," said William.

Norris focused on the screen.

"There…"

Now Norris saw them. Three of them.

"They are in his brain stem," said William.

"What is that?" asked the technician, alarmed.

Norris grabbed William's arm. "How do we get them out?" he asked, whispering.

William looked him in the eye. "I'm not sure." He turned to the technician. "Quickly, keep scanning."

Norris didn't understand what the hurry was.

The scan continued.

"Oh, my goodness," said the technician.

Norris peered into the screen. The color of the brain changed from white to red, then to yellow, and finally blue.

"What is that?" Norris demanded.

William was staring at him. "We need to secure Mr. Murphy."

A loud shriek startled them. They turned and noticed Nicholas was gone. The door burst open, and Nicholas's red eyes glared at them. His face was white as a ghost, pasty, showed no fear, no emotion.

"Nicholas?" muttered Norris.

Norris reached for his gun, but Nicholas was fast and threw himself on the technician, biting the man's hand.

"No!" William cried out and pulled Nicholas away.

But he was too strong. He jabbed William and grabbed his neck.

"Nicholas, stop!" yelled Norris.

He was about to strangle him when Norris pulled the trigger. The shot echoed and blood oozed out of Nicholas's chest. His eyes rolled up, and he collapsed.

Norris moved back; his eyes remained fixed on the lifeless body of his friend.

County Morgue

Five lives were lost, and the recent one was lying on the steel table in front of William. The horrifying experience haunted him. He hated himself for not figuring it out soon. It might have saved Nicholas. William didn't bother to call Fredrick.

Putting his fears and his pain aside, he got ready for another autopsy. He wanted to find out if the nanobots inside Nicholas were identical to the ones he had found in Daisy.

He couldn't help but wonder. Was it just Nicholas and Daisy? How did it enter their bodies? Nicholas was fine in the hospital, a bit off, but he had just lost his family. What triggered it? The magnets in the MRI machine? No. If it were metallic, it would have ripped it out of his body, probably killing him as soon as the scan began. Possibly the killer was on to them. Perhaps the killer realized they had discovered the nanobots and decided to act.

Once more, he checked the full-body scans of Nicholas. The nanobots were only in his brain. William picked up the scalpel and began his work.

The brain was usually the last organ he would dissect, but today that was where he started.

At 3 am, he held the part of Nicholas's cerebellum in his hands. Gently, he pierced through the tissue. In the middle of the brain stem, he saw it. He took in a deep breath, almost worried that it might come to life. With trembling fingers, he reached for the nanobot and placed it in a container.

After he had collected all the nanobots, he reexamined the body. The lacerations on Nicholas's hands were recent. Other than that, there were no wounds or signs of an injection, but then they might have healed. Just like Daisy, William did not know when the nanobots entered his system. It could have been months or even years.

William was done collecting samples. Now it was time to send them off to Juliet.

He was on his way to the post office when he heard a commotion. A group of villagers stood in front of the sheriff's office. Two of the deputies were talking with them, but the villagers appeared agitated. William paid no heed and kept walking to his destination.

By the time William finished, the crowd had left. He entered the sheriff's office.

"What happened?"

"Nothing."

"Are you sure?"

Norris shook his head. "I shot Nicholas. That is going to have consequences."

"But he was going to kill us."

"We know that. But the villagers don't. They were devoted to him. This will not go down well."

William walked toward him. "Look, I get it. These people are close, and they are feeling lost, confused, and angry. But we have a bigger problem. We need to find out if others were injected with the nanobots."

"How do we find out?"

"We can't scan everyone. How about looking at their medical history?"

"How would that help?"

"The nanobots cannot be inhale. If swallowed, I do not think they would go past the digestive system."

"Why?"

"Because our digestive system has acids, that break down food to be converted into energy. Whatever it determines unnecessary is thrown out of the body."

"So, if it had to stay out of the digestive system... then how would it enter the brain?"

"It had to be injected."

"That would be painful."

"It would be, and you know what? People would remember pain."

"Or they might have been unconscious when it was done."

"That means a loss of time—people would remember that too."

35

DRONES AND TASERS

16th February 2020 (Present day)
Mayor's House

Ms. Pritchard and the children finished assembling the drones. William and Tom returned and began loading the tasers onto the drones.

Installing the tasers was easy. The drones were built to carry spraying tubes, and William and Tom were replacing them with tasers as fast as possible.

William was feeling tired. It was nearing 2 am. It was silent now; he didn't know if that was a good or a bad sign. He was afraid to look out through the window.

William positioned the last taser on the drone and ran his hand through his head. Finally, after hours of work, it was done. He thought of Norris and wondered where he was.

He should be here. We need him.

"Okay, what now?" Tom asked William.

The teacher and the children returned to the basement. They entered the study. William paused when he saw Jack and Roumoult on the video call. Roumoult was still on the phone.

"What's happening?" William asked.

"We are trying to get you help!" Jack replied.

"That would be good," William said, and then focused on the task. "Are the drones online?"

"Initiating now," Jack answered.

They waited.

On one screen they saw the nanobots all over the village, and most of them were around the town center.

"Oh, damn…" Jack said.

"What now?"

"The signal strength is low. If we want to control them remotely, I need the signal to be strong."

William threw his hands in the air. "What do we need to do now?"

After fifteen minutes of discussing their options, they decided to place the booster on the network tower past the town hall. William was reluctant to put himself or Tom in any more danger, but his plan relied on the drones.

"We are heading off," he told Jack and spotted Roumoult standing silently with his head bowed. "Listen, as soon as we get to the tower, activate the drones. Okay?"

Jack's face turned grim. "The drones cannot differentiate between you and the zombies! You might get hurt!"

Tom and William looked at each other.

"We'll take our chances. Are you sure you and Fredrick can handle the drones?"

"Yes."

"I wish you would wait," Roumoult intervened.

"We can't," William argued.

William didn't want to leave the children, Ms. Pritchard and Fredrick unguarded, but this was a two-man job.

"Lock the door and do not open it at any cost," he told Fredrick.

As they left the house, he checked his gun. Tom walked along with him.

"Can we take the car?"

"No. That would attract attention."

Tom shook his head. "The tower is almost a mile away near the town center."

"I know," William answered, putting the heavy bag on his back.

William was glad to slow down when they arrived at a cluster of houses. He was breathing hard, sweat dripped down his neck, and he was dizzy. William didn't know how long he could keep this up. The cold, the slippery road and the bag were not making it easy.

Tom caught up with him. After a brief break, they started jogging again. They paused when they heard screams and shouts. The fire was still raging; it had spread to the forest. Smoke and ash filled the air. They were nearing chaos.

Staying out of sight, they neared the center of the town. William assessed their situation. Several lifeless bodies laid on the ground in awkward positions. Blood smeared the mud, and the rotten smell of flesh prickled his nostrils. He waited, but the shadows didn't appear.

"Let's go."

William and Tom circled around the town center, using the thick forest as a cover. They stopped once in a while to make sure they weren't being followed. Even if one zombie saw them, it would alert the others. As they moved to their destination, William noticed two silent and dark houses.

After their long, tiring jog, they reached the tower. William looked up. It appeared to touch the sky and was broad at the base and narrow at the top. It stood on a thick cement platform.

"Where should we place the booster?"

"As high as possible," replied William.

Without further delay, they began climbing. As they moved up the ladder, William came upon a locked circular door. He struck the bolt with the back of his gun and broke it.

The climb was hard and tiring. He had to stop several times. The wind was chilly, and the fog was becoming thicker. He looked down and saw Tom was falling behind.

At the top of the tower was a triangular platform. Four large satellite dishes faced each direction. He stood for a moment and observed the entire village, the swamp, and the mountain.

Breathless, he took a moment and then began. William held the booster as Tom fixed its legs using a drill. Once they were done, they turned it on.

William called Jack. "Check now."

"Okay. Wait," Jack replied, "Well, we are good to go. Get back here as soon as possible."

William felt a weight of him. Without the booster on his back, the climb down was easier and faster. Even so, he was weary.

"You okay," Tom asked.

"Let's just get this done," he said.

Staying away from the crazy crowd, they moved back in the direction of the mayor's house. They were en route when William paused. From inside one of the houses, he heard cries. Tom came to a stop beside him. Two children not over two years old stepped out of the house crying.

"Mommy! Mommy!"

"Oh, my god!" Tom cried out.

William was about to rush toward them when a man appeared out of nowhere and grabbed a kid.

36

TRUTH AND LIES

14th February 2020
Sheriff's Office

The hospital was a very unsettling place to work, so William got the files he needed and came to the sheriff's office. He sat in a corner, going through one file after another. The deputies joked, played card games, and ate peanuts. One of them kept coming and peering into the medical records.

Several surgical procedures were carried out at the hospital over the past five years. He did not know what he was looking for. Most of them had been cuts, falls, and bruises requiring stitches or casts. They rarely performed neurological exams or tests. Most of the people in the village were in good health, and the local doctors had to handle minor medical issues, such as anemia or vitamin deficiencies.

Meadow Cottage

Both men returned home on time. Norris had a small dinner and continued working. William poured himself a glass of brandy and started working on the laptop on the dining table.

Time passed painfully. William remained silent as he flipped through the reports. The words and numbers made no sense to him. He figured William would tell him eventually.

15th February 2020

When he felt tired, he headed off to bed. Norris didn't remember when he slept. When he opened his eyes, the room was bright, and full of smell of fresh coffee.

Norris brushed, shaved, and showered and then came downstairs to find William making breakfast. The dinning table was covered with papers, notes and printouts.

"Hey, morning." William said.

"Morning," replied Norris, "Did you sleep?"

"Yes, a little."

Norris stood with his arms folded, looking at the table.

William placed two plates on the coffee table. "Just for today," William said.

"I hope so," Norris replied. "I like to have my breakfast on this table."

William eyed him. "Sure. I'll keep that in mind. I am in the middle of something. As soon as I am done, I'll clean it up."

Norris nodded, and they ate in silence.

William's phone rang a few times; Norris noted it was Joan calling.

"Aren't you going to pick that up?" Norris said.

"I'm not sure what to say to her?" William said.

"What is she asking?" Norris asked.

"She wants me to come back. She thinks I am not safe here."

"She is right."

"Many things... have happened... and they make you question everything."

"What happened?"

"Since the pandemic started, everything has changed."

"Are you sure the pandemic had anything to do with it?"

William looked at him. "I think this situation is putting too much pressure on our relationship."

"Hm... I am sure you two are fine."

"Maybe we weren't supposed to be together."

"How did you get together?"

"For that I blame Roumoult."

Norris laughed. "Really?"

"He kept pushing me to date her..."

"Ah... you weren't interested?"

"I liked her, but I was getting over a nasty breakup."

"Well, you can't put it all on Roumoult, you must have felt something for her."

William hung his head. "She is something. I really really like her."

"How is the sex?"

"Amazing."

"Okay, so you have great careers, you have exciting times. You have amazing sex, and yet..."

"She is so controlling."

"Like?"

"She makes me eat salad."

"That's good for you in the long-term. She cares."

"She monitors me all the time."

"Meaning?"

"Well. If I am late or hanging out with my friends, she calls."

"Have you disappeared or been in danger before?"

William became thoughtful. "Well, once someone kidnapped me and put me in a coffin."

"That explains her behavior. How about your friends? Are they involved in any dangerous activities?"

"You know us right. We are always solving mysteries…"

Norris smirked. "William, she is worried you might get into trouble… so she keeps tabs on you."

"Well. It makes me uncomfortable."

"Tell her."

"What if she gets mad?"

"Tell her nicely."

William sat silently for a moment. "That is not the only thing. But I am wondering, where this is going?"

"Oh, you don't see a future?"

"I see the future… I don't know if she sees the same one."

County Morgue

In the coroner's office, the bodies lay undisturbed. William was getting edgy. He hadn't heard from Juliet or Jack. It was possible they hadn't finished their work.

He concentrated on the corpses. They were voiceless. They couldn't tell him who killed them, about their death, or their suffering. It seemed as if he was unraveling their stories, their mysteries. The laptop beeped. A video call came through, and William answered.

"What are you doing in the morgue?" asked Roumoult in an authoritative tone.

"Hi. How are you? Nice to see you too."

"William, don't mock me."

"What's with the mood?"

"You lied to me!"

William became alert.

"So this case you are working on involves an organization that has created nanobots that turn people into murderers and psychopaths!"

William smiled. "Excellent deduction."

"William! Are you nuts?"

"Are you done?"

Roumoult ran his hand through his hair. "Who else is involved?"

"Ah, Tom, and Jack."

Roumoult rolled his eyes. "Any leads?"

"On the people who created it? No. But we are getting close."

The screen split in two, and Jack's face materialized.

"Jack! You told Roumoult," William scolded.

"Well, William, you are his friend. I am his employee and his friend. There is a difference!"

William scowled.

"He was going to find out, anyway!"

William shook his head. "Did you find anything about the logo on the nanobot?"

"Nope. But I studied it further. Its purpose was to travel to a certain point and then attach itself to the tissues and remain there until further instructions. It also has a transmitter."

"Further instructions? I don't like the sound of that," Roumoult interposed.

William rubbed his head, got on his feet, and walked around the room. "I think there are more people with nanobots inside them."

"Is there a way to identify them?" Roumoult asked.

"No. The bots might have entered their bodies via a lumbar puncture, infusion, an injection... it could be subcutaneous."

"Stop. You are giving me a headache," Roumoult said.

William gaped at him.

"If this was, let's say, an illegal project, there wouldn't be records of a lumbar puncture... or any kind of procedure. It would be recorded as something harmless or completely unrelated to any procedures."

William's face turned to stone. "They would lie to people!"

"Everyone lies," Roumoult remarked.

William rubbed his temples.

"Let us assume they wanted to test people. One or two might not be enough. If I were you, I would ask around if anyone has tested the villagers in groups. Like a vaccination camp. If the answer is no, then it was probably only Daisy and her family. If the answer is yes, you might have a bigger problem. And perhaps it's time to call the NYPD."

Sheriff's Office

The phone rang again, and Norris thought his day couldn't get worse. Guilt clouded his mind. Nicholas and his family were dead, and it was his fault. He wondered if he should have handled it differently.

He had killed his friend. He didn't need a reminder that he had done something wrong. It wouldn't bring him back. Norris wanted to find out why his friend turned. What triggered it?

The shot rang in his head, and tears gathered in his eyes. He could not handle his sorrow, and it was spreading throughout the village. He sensed the bitterness, mistrust, and fear amongst the villagers.

The door to his office opened, and Mayor Henry Rogers walked. Norris frowned.

"We need to talk," the mayor said.

Norris folded his arms while he took a seat.

"The villagers are upset."

"I am aware."

"You need to talk with them."

"I thought that was your job."

"It's about Nicholas."

Norris's heart sank. A sense of guilt, despair, and grief ran through his veins. He never thought one day he would have to kill his childhood friend. He didn't need anyone else heckling him.

"I did what I had to do," Norris replied, almost

choking.

Henry nodded. "I'm aware of that. We need to address the situation."

"I know. I am trying to understand what happened to Nicholas and his family."

"He just lost it. His daughter is dead, his wife gone… he just lost it, Norris."

"I want to find out the truth."

"The people don't care about the truth."

"I care!"

Henry fell silent.

"What do you want from me?"

"I think you should apologize for your behavior."

Norris raised an eyebrow. "Apologize for what? For doing my job?"

"Of course not. I get it. Just say it was an unfortunate situation. Tell them how you feel. Nicholas's death is a substantial loss to our community, and we have to arrange a conference."

Norris nodded. "Of course, we do, but first we need to get answers and make sure this doesn't happen again."

"Well, right now, the villagers are agitated. Angry. They want answers. They want answers from the M. E and they want to find out what he has discovered so far. He sends parcels after parcels to the city. What's in them? What were the results? The people need to know."

"Talking of secrets, you've got a few of your own."

Henry's face turned grim.

"Why do you have a Phoneutria? One of the most dangerous spiders in the world."

The mayor remained silent.

"Were you aware of the illegal dump in the swamp that Lauren was investigating?"

Henry sat back in the chair.

"Lauren, the journalist who visited Nightridge six months ago. We found her body in the swamp."

"Norris…"

"We traced her calls, and you were one of the last people she spoke with."

Henry gulped. "Nicholas's death has nothing to do with these things."

"I wonder, where have you been for the last three nights?"

Blood drained from Henry's face. "That's none of your business."

"Where is Charlotte? Henry, where is your wife?"

"She went to her mother's."

"Really, I thought there was a lockdown… and no one is traveling. Why did she leave? Where is Charlotte?"

Henry stood up. "You do not tell me what to do! I have called a conference at the town hall, and you are going to speak to the people."

"Sure. Should I also share your secrets?"

Henry's face turned red, and he marched out of the office.

That was all Norris needed. He picked up the phone and called Tom.

Town Hall

The conference room in the town hall was not a a grand place. Norris stood on the platform and waited for everyone to settle down. When the room turned silent, he noticed several men and women but no children. Fredrick and William stood in a corner. Deputies Kyle and Hector stood near the podium. The lights were dull, the night freezing and dark with a heavy fog descending on the village.

"Thank you for coming today," Norris said, glancing toward the mayor. "We have had a really testing time. The pandemic has taken away our freedom, our loved ones, changed our lives, and forced us to hide away in our houses. It has also raised fear, concern and anger." He paused. "Nicholas was... one of the few good people I knew. He was a father, a husband, a provider, and most of all, my friend."

Norris paused again. He didn't think he could continue, but he couldn't stop now. "It... it breaks my heart. I should have thought of a better way to handle him. But I just reacted. He had already lost his wife, his daughter, and was under a lot of stress. But he was beside himself. He attacked a technician at the hospital, and I wished I could have done things differently... but..."

"You shouldn't have shot him!" shouted a man.

"I shouldn't have... but he wasn't Nicholas anymore."

"He was sick, scared, and alone!" said a woman.

"I understand."

"No. You don't! You don't just gun down someone like that!"

"What did you think I should have done?"

"Shot him in the leg," argued the woman.

"Try to understand him! Reason with him," yelled another woman.

Norris bit his lips. "I should have... but I couldn't."

"I think you should answer for your actions."

"Now. Now," Henry said, raising his hands. "We are here not to blame anyone. It was a tragedy, and I am sorry. But the sheriff is right. It is his duty to protect, and he did his best."

Norris was amazed. He thought Henry would crush him in front of these people.

"We need to prevent this from happening again. And we must stay calm."

"We agree," added Norris. "I think for everyone's safety, all villagers should give up their firearms..."

Henry glared at him.

"What the fuck are you talking about!" screamed a man.

"Are you mad?" shrieked another.

"Why should we leave ourselves undefended? You should give up your gun! You are the one who shot Nicholas!" called out a villager.

"It all began in a house that had a gun. Daisy shot her mom, then she attacked her father. It could happen again, to any of us..."

"I don't believe this. You can't ask us to do that!" argued a woman.

"I know, such a hypocrite!" exclaimed another villager.

"It's just a precaution," said Norris. He noticed William appearing concerned.

"Go to hell! You have no right to do that!" said a man.

"He doesn't," said Henry. "What he is trying to say is, let's be cautious until we have more answers."

"Yes. Yes. We want answers!" said a villager. He turned to William. "What did you find out?" he demanded.

William exchanged glances with Norris. "It's complicated and we are still investigating."

"Do you think I am stupid?"

William's face reddened. "No. It's not like that. I wouldn't want to make a statement until I know what we are dealing with here."

"So, Sheriff… the smart man you got from the city knows nothing about what happened to Nicholas and his family!" screamed a woman.

Norris frowned. "What he means, he is still investigating. Finding answers. Do you want us to make false statements? What if we are wrong?"

"Oh, you are just making excuses!"

"I don't believe this," muttered Norris. "Everyone. Please calm down. We have to make sure no one else gets hurt."

"Oh… we will make sure of that. You just stay out of our way!" exclaimed a man, walking out of the conference room.

"Rick… Rick…" called out Henry.

Norris and William exchanged worried glances. The atmosphere in the conference room changed. People were arguing, talking loudly, and then a couple of women started fighting. Billy walked to the front and punched a villager.

"Stop it!" shouted Norris.

Billy didn't, and he attacked another man. Two deputies and Norris grabbed Billy and shoved him away.

Billy glared at Norris. All around them, villagers were screaming and arguing over trifle matters.

It took over half an hour for the sheriff, cops and the mayor to stop the arguments. But the rage was unmistakable, and most of the villagers left yelling profanities.

They exchanged troubled glances.

"What the hell was that?" demanded William.

"I don't know," said Norris.

"I don't believe it… they are usually so…" Kyle said.

"Peaceful, calm, understanding, and harmless," said Norris.

"Tonight, they're out of control," William pointed out.

"Henry, perhaps you can shed some light on this matter," said Norris.

The mayor gaped at him, and without another word, he left.

The deputies stayed back, and so did Fredrick.

"I need to ask you something," said William. "Has anything happened in the last year?"

"The pandemic," replied Hector.

"Ah, nothing that dynamic. Something clinical when people were treated in groups."

"Like a vaccination camp?" Kyle asked.

"Something like that. A medical event… maybe sponsored from someone outside the village."

"Oh yes. There was a medical camp," Kyle confirmed.

"When was that?"

"I think eight months ago."

"Why didn't I know about it?" asked Norris.

"You were out-of-town visiting your daughter. The mayor approved it."

"What did it involve?" William asked.

"Medical camps are very common down here. We do not have a lot of facilities, and many of the villagers do not have medical insurance and are hard on cash," explained Norris.

"Chief, it was the usual camp we run every year. The medical tests, the doctors' examinations… everything was the same… except the shot," Kyle said.

"What shot?" asked William.

"The multivitamin shot. They told us that vitamin deficiency was very common in the village."

All eyes turned to Kyle.

"How many people were involved in this camp?" Norris asked.

"Everyone except the children."

Norris couldn't believe his ears.

37

NO STOPPING IT NOW

16th February 2020 (Present day)
Nightridge

William's heart raced as he ran to save the children. The man was about to break the child's neck when Tom knocked him down. William picked up the weeping children and moved away from the fight. The man snarled, scrawled, got back on his feet, and was about to attack when Tom kicked him to the ground and knocked him out.

Hugging the kids, William said, "It's okay. I got you… it's okay."

"Mommy… I want my mommy."

William had no time. They rushed toward the mayor's home. Suddenly, William stopped dead on his feet. From within, the shadow's figures emerged.

"Oh, dear lord," muttered Tom.

A group of men with guns and axes were blocking their path. Billy stood in front of the group and glared at Tom with a devilish smile.

"I wondered where you were hiding?" Billy said, smiling.

William was shocked. He didn't know if people could talk under the influence of the nanobots.

"This can't be good," mumbled Tom.

William turned and ran in the other direction. The children moaned in his arms. His heart rate kept climbing, and he was breathless. His leg muscles were strained, and his arms were sore. He glanced behind, relieved they weren't following. They just stood there, watching.

"Whoa!" cried out Tom.

They stopped.

Another group of men and women stood in front of them, watching. Waiting. William swung to their right, and faces emerged from the darken windows of the houses. Behind the houses, the fire raged and was spreading into the forest. They would never make it out of here. The children cried, and William held them close. They were surrounded.

Tom armed himself.

"How many can you take out?"

"Few. I can buy you and the kids some time. Go!"

"I am not leaving you!"

"You have no choice."

"Tom, they will kill you…"

William was about to reply, but paused. From every

direction, the villagers slowly began moving toward them. The two men huddled together. William bit his lips, trying to think of a way of getting out. Then he heard a loud whizzing. William turned, and from within the pitch-black forest appeared red lights.

38

A PRICE MUST BE PAID

15th February 2020
County Morgue

L ife Savers, a nonprofit organization, had sponsored the medical camp. Medical professionals hired by them had visited the village every year for the last ten years. On paper, William couldn't find anything unusual. He went through staff files.

All the staff members were well qualified and authentic. The reports were filed with precision. Kyle was right; 90 percent of the population had deficiencies in vitamin K, D, B12 and magnesium. A multivitamin shot would help, but he personally preferred long-term treatment. He wondered if there were copies of the prescription. He didn't find any.

Then he watched a few videos about the camp. He was

quite tired and couldn't keep his eyes open as the final footage of the camp played.

The phone rang, and Tom's concerned face emerged on the screen.

"Hey... how are you?" William asked.

"I am alright. I am alright..."

William swallowed hard.

"What happened?" Tom asked.

William updated the detective about Nicholas and the villagers' rage.

"This is getting ugly."

"I know. Tom, we need help."

"I'll see what I can do."

"Another thing. I need you to run background checks on the medical team that visited Nightridge."

After an hour, William got ready to leave for home. As he stood up and picked up his jacket, his phone rang. It was Tom.

"That was fast," Tom said.

"I had nothing much to do. All the staff check out except one. Her name in the medical file is Ann Finn. But the Ann Finn on records was born and lived in Washington for most of her life. She has been working as a nurse since 1978. Married and moved to New York six years ago."

He showed her a picture of a much older woman with short gray hair and black glasses.

"So, someone stole her identity to be at that camp."

"Yep."

"What is her actual name?"

"Lara Green. She was born and brought up in the Bronx. Lara was a nurse for several years in a local clinic but was fired for stealing drugs and interacting inappropriately with the patients."

William folded his arms.

"Her registration has expired, her bank accounts are non-existent, she has no social security number, and our records show she was living with her mother in Queens."

"Alright."

"I have sent some officers to check it out… but for now, we do not know where she is."

William nodded and contemplated. Could Ann have injected the nanobots? But why and who was she working for?

15th February 2020

Mayor's Home

Norris followed his instincts and followed the mayor to his home. Norris shut the door of the truck as the lights in the house came to life. He banged his fist on the door.

"What do you want?" Henry demanded, opening the door.

"Answers!"

"I have got nothing!"

"I am not so sure about that! Only one person could have authorized that camp in my absence, and that was you!"

"I don't know what you are talking about."

"Did you take part?"

"I don't need to tell you anything. Get out!"

A bell grabbed Norris's attention, and he noticed the study door was ajar. Without warning, he barged in.

"You can't go in there!"

He froze. In front of him were three screens showing graphs. They reminded him of the ECG monitors in the hospital. The moving lines were peaking and dipping, as if tracking something.

"What is this?"

"None of your business."

But Norris knew already. In the screen's corner was the three-drop logo. To his left was a server, similar to the lab on the mountain.

"You did this," he said, facing him.

"I say…"

Henry didn't finish his sentence. Norris grabbed his neck. "What the hell is this? What did you do?"

"Go to hell."

"Well, that won't be a problem!" Norris punched him in the face. "I am prepared for it." He grabbed Henry and pushed him against the wall. "What did you do?"

"It's done! You can't stop it! Your hot shot M. E from the city can't do anything now. You brought him here thinking you can solve this. You are an idiot if you think you are smarter than me."

"I am not smarter than you, but I am stronger!"

"You are a pussy!"

Norris controlled his anger. "Tell me what you did!"

"Go figure it out."

Norris took a shot and said, "You worked with

Sanders to develop this technology. You gave them permission to dig in the mountain. And then when he pulled out of the project, you secretly kept developing it. Then you arranged for the camp, purposely, when I wasn't around. You injected everyone with the nanobots. Your own people! Your friends! The men and women who supported you! Why? Why the hell would you do this?"

"You wouldn't understand!"

Norris jabbed him. "Try me!"

"They need to pay!"

"Who!"

"This godforsaken country... the government... Everyone!"

Norris's eyes widened, and he released the grip on Henry's neck.

"Oh, no. Not because of Jeffery."

"Why should the common man's child live when my son died? Why should they have families when my family is gone! They took my son! They murdered him!"

"No. It was the virus!"

"No! It was them! They neglected his condition and my son choked to death. They did nothing to save him. Nothing! He died alone, afraid, surrounded by strangers. And they did nothing! NOTHING to save him! They have to pay! They have to pay!"

"You've lost your mind!"

"No."

"You have killed five people already."

"No, I didn't. I liberated them."

"They are people."

"Daisy was the best. She was the first and the best. Oh, wow… her results were fantastic."

Norris couldn't believe his ears.

"Nicholas was a bit of a disappointment because you killed him before I could study all the stages."

"All the stages?" Norris said. He grabbed his collar. "What do you mean?"

Henry smiled devilishly. "First, they sleepwalk. Do things they don't remember. They might walk alone… barefoot in the forest. Then they turned violent. Monsters, who attack people, kill for no reason."

"I don't believe this," Norris said, shaking his head.

"The third step is the best. They turn into zombies. Mindless souls… who hunt… hunt and kill everyone!"

"What the hell did you do?"

The monitor beeped. The lines remained straight.

"What is that?"

"It reads their brains. And I have control."

Norris's face turned to stone.

"They are my puppets. I will take my revenge. Sanders wanted to create a neurological tool to heal. I wanted the perfect weapon to kill. When he withdrew, I kept the lab and persuaded a scientist to build the next version."

Norris's jaw fell. "This is why you killed Lauren."

"She knew very little, but it was enough to alert the authorities."

"You are crazy!"

"Maybe. I will liberate people… force them to stand up for me. Not bend to anyone's will. No one should have died in this pandemic. No one!"

"Where is your wife?" Norris demanded.

"No one stands in my way anymore, not even her."

Norris was astonished. "You were not the only one who lost someone!"

"I am surprised. I thought you would be on my side. You are a coward! A pussy! You lost your son and your grandson... and yet you defend them."

"I defend this village and its people."

"I know that... and you will die defending these ungrateful cunts!"

Norris heard a click behind him. With a heavy heart, he turned and saw Hector pointing a gun at him.

"Sorry, Chief, you know too much."

"Of course, you would need a cop to cover the murders," Norris said as he turned to glare at Henry, "but you won't be able to cover mass murder."

"You mean your friend from New York? What makes you think he will make it out alive?"

County Morgue

William decided not to go home and do an internet search on Ann Green. The problem was he found too many women with the same name.

A loud cry echoed down the hall. He jumped, and he rushed out to find Fredrick standing, glaring at something.

"What is it?"

But Fredrick remained frozen, staring at something in the darkness.

William followed his gaze. It was foggy, silent. Too

quiet, he noticed. The village was usually peaceful, but noises made by television or stereos and people chatting were very common. But now it was dead silent.

"Jesus…" Fredrick muttered.

William had to strain, and in the shadow's, he saw it. It was a figure, still as a statue. A man, medium built, about his height.

"It's just a man," William said.

Fredrick pointed to his left. William saw another figure. Still as stone.

"Hello!" shouted William

"Don't do that! Something is off. Something is not right with them."

They waited, but the figures didn't move.

Fredrick tried to stop him, but William crossed the small meadow and slowly neared the first figure. As he stepped closer, he noticed it was one villager he had seen in the conference room.

"Excuse me, are you alright?" he asked almost in a whisper.

He could feel Fredrick shivering behind him. William tapped the man's shoulder. He didn't move.

"Hello there," William said, waving his hand in front of his eyes. He didn't blink.

"What happened to him?" Fredrick asked.

"I don't know," William said, casually checking the man's pulse. He was alive. He turned toward the second figure. It was a woman he had seen around in the village. Her eyes wide-open, and she was breathing but stood still.

"What's happening?" William muttered.

"I have no idea. We have to find the sheriff," muttered Fredrick.

Mayor's home

"Are you really going to do this?" Norris said to Hector, "Have you realized the consequences of your actions? You are responsible for everyone who dies tonight!"

"The mayor will protect me."

"Are you sure about that? He's out of his senses! He's delusional!"

"Don't listen to him..." Henry yelled.

Norris surprised Hector by punching him in the stomach. The gun fell from Hector's hand and slid away. Hector charged toward him, and Norris kicked him in the groin. Hector cried out, dropping to the floor.

"Stupid man!" Norris grumbled. He made him stand and cuffed him to the radiator.

Henry rushed toward the door, but Norris seized him and shoved him to the floor.

"Shut it down!"

"No!"

Norris gripped him by the collar. "Shut it down," he yelled, kicking him.

Henry whimpered in pain.

"Shut it down or I swear on the grave of my son and grandson, I'll bury you right here."

"I can't."

Norris was about to hit him again, but the major flinched and cried out.

"No. No. No more. I can't take it! I can't shut it down. It has a default system."

Norris didn't believe him.

"There is no shutting it down," Henry said.

Norris studied the monitor. The lines were still flat. "What do those lines mean?"

"I activated the nanobots. They are immobile, for now."

"Immobile?"

"Yes. But once those lines move... the levels of the brain waves will increase and slowly they will become more and more aggressive."

Norris teared up. "What the hell is wrong with you?"

"Why don't you understand? You ignorant man! They have to pay! Those criminals need to pay! They could have stopped this!"

"No one could have stopped it," muttered Norris, and knocked him out.

His eyes then shifted to the monitors. It showed 45 minutes. What did that mean? Perhaps by the time he had left. Could he call NYPD? Could they get here in time? He didn't know. His phone rang.

Town Center

William didn't even stop to breathe as they ran toward the mayor's home. Every person he saw in the village was motionless, immobile, as if time had stopped. He paused when he heard noises from the school. He and Fredrick exchanged glances and rushed toward the building.

They bashed open the door and raced down the empty corridor. They followed the noises and entered an enormous hall. Ms. Pritchard and over twenty children were busy painting pictures. She looked up when she saw them.

"What's wrong?" Ms. Pritchard asked.

"You are alright?" said William.

She looked confused.

"Yeah... What's happening, Fredrick?"

"Didn't you go to the medical camp?"

Ms. Pritchard looked confused. "What camp?"

"It happened over eight months ago," Fredrick said.

"Eight months. I wasn't here. I was taking care of my nana."

Both men exchanged glances.

"What is going on?" she asked, alarmed.

"Stay indoors."

She waited for answers. William didn't want to frighten her.

"Something is going on. Is there a place you and the children could hide?"

She glanced at the children worriedly.

"Trust me, I will come and check on you. Do you know of a good place to hide?"

"There is an old basement in this building. Only a few people know about it," she replied.

"Good. Let's do that first."

. . .

After ensuring the children and the teacher were safe, they left the building. As they made their way to the mayor's house, they checked a few houses. They entered a house where the door was open to find a couple watching TV, sitting like statues. The children were asleep in their rooms.

Soon they reached the mayor's house. Norris stood at the door. Huffing, William explained to him what was happening.

"Everyone?" he asked.

"Yes. Except us and the children."

"This can't be good," Norris said.

They heard footsteps. Norris pulled his gun.

"Chief, it's me!" Kyle said, raising his hands.

"Why aren't you..."

"Like them? I-I don't know. What is happening? I saw William and Fredrick running toward this house and followed them."

"Did you get the shot?" Norris asked.

Kyle became silent.

"Tell the truth."

"I hate needles. I lied, chief. I didn't take the shot!"

"Lucky you," muttered Norris.

They entered the house, and William closed the door behind them. William noticed Norris had cuffed Hector to the radiator, and Henry sat in a corner with his hands tied and a gag in his mouth.

"Ah, what's going on?" William asked Norris.

After hearing the entire ordeal, William felt like kicking Henry himself. However, he controlled himself.

"We need to turn it off..." Norris said, pointing toward the monitor.

"You can't!" screamed Henry.

"Shut up!" shouted both William and Norris.

Norris and Kyle took the mayor and Hector to the basement. They tied and gagged them, then stepped away. Hector remained silent, but Henry kept trying to yell.

Norris looked at him. "You have got what you wanted. They are turning. And if they are anything like Daisy or Nicholas, pray we find a way to shut the nanobots down. Because if we die, just imagine what they would do to you. They might just eat you alive. Tear you apart or kill you bit by bit."

Color drained from Henry's face.

Norris returned upstairs with Kyle and found William and Jack conversing on the phone.

"This program is monitoring nanobots. You see these lines going up and down. These are probably brain waves."

"Oh, this is incredible. Can we shut it down?" asked Fredrick.

"I don't know. I have to find how the software is controlling the nanobots."

"How can you do that?" Fredrick asked.

"I can access the server remotely. What's the hurry?"

"Um. Let me see. All the villagers except these five people are frozen."

"Frozen?"

"Yeah. If we don't shut that thing down, they are going to start moving... and then become mindless, violent people."

"You mean like zombies?" concluded Jack.

"Jack. Find a way to deactivate the bots!"

Jack looked frazzled. "Fredrick, I am sending you a link. Download the software so I can take over the computer remotely."

"Okay," Fredrick replied, grabbing a chair.

"What should we do?" Kyle asked.

"We have to neutralize the nanobots without killing the villagers," instructed William.

"And call the NYPD... we need help," said Norris.

County Morgue

Trying not to break the new hand-held optical scanner, William walked hurriedly. Kyle was carrying the monitor while William turned on the probe. Approaching the paralyzed man, William placed the scanner at the base of the head. Kyle switched on the machine. The machine beeped, and soon images emerged.

"Why are we wasting time?" muttered Norris.

"Wait," William said.

They saw three objects sitting close to the brain stem.

William moved to the other regions of the brain. Brain activity had diminished.

"They have attached themselves to the brain and may emit some kind of signal that has disabled other brain activity."

"Incredible," muttered Kyle.

"How can they stand for so long—don't their legs pain?" asked Norris.

"All the pain centers are connected with the brain. As far as I know, they may feel nothing. They are not thinking. And god knows what they will do when they wake up."

"Or the venom in the nanobots might just kill them."

"We have about thirty minutes," Kyle said. "we should act fast."

William nodded and stopped scanning. He rushed toward the morgue and searched through the medicine cabinet, checking every bottle.

"What are you doing?" Norris asked.

William found a syringe and filled it.

"What's that?"

"Xanax."

"What does it do?" Norris asked.

William didn't answer and hurried out of the morgue. Without hesitating, he pushed the syringe into the woman's arm. There was no pain, and in seconds, she dropped to the ground.

"What did you do?"

"Gave her a sedative that would put a horse to sleep."

"For how long?"

"I don't know."

"We can't leave her out here. What if others wake up and hurt her?" said Norris.

They carried the lady and locked her in the room of one of the neighboring houses.

"Okay… this might work," Kyle said.

They returned to the morgue, and William prepared another injection.

"It might be a long shot. Remember, once the nanobots are activated, there is no telling what will happen."

They injected the man, who fell on the ground stiff like a mannequin.

"Any side effects?" Norris asked.

"Headaches, dizziness, and vomiting," William answered.

"Well, better than turning into a zombie," Norris remarked.

"We can't run around the entire village injecting people," Kyle pointed out.

"We have to find a different way of administering this drug," William spoke.

"Whatever happens, we cannot let them leave the village… do you understand? We can't let them leave," Norris said.

"Well… the only way out is the bridge," Kyle remarked.

Their eyes met.

William's phone rang; it was Jack.

"What happened?" William asked.

"I need to show you guys something," Jack stated.

. . .

They returned to the house and found a very nervous Fredrick. On one screen were several green dots.

"If I am not mistaken, on this monitor we can see the location of all the nanobots."

"You mean... people," Norris corrected him.

"Yeah."

"Have you found the frequency?"

"That is hard. Whoever created this had a false safe system."

"Password?"

"Passwords. Several of them."

"Break them!" shouted Norris.

"That takes time..."

"Something is happening," Kyle said, pointing to the screen.

The dots began moving.

"Sheriff!" shouted Fredrick.

They peered through the window and saw a man step out of the house.

"Turn off the lights! We have to make sure they don't see us," said William.

Kyle acted fast and flipped the switch.

The room turned dark, and they watched in silence. He just stood there. Soon two women appeared.

William shut his eyes. "Jack. Can you do anything? Can we control them?"

"I don't know... I don't think anyone can control them."

"We have to come up with..." Norris's voice trailed away.

The man hit the woman and began strangling her.

Another woman screeched and bit the man, who squealed and hit her hard with his elbow. He picked up an ax and swung it, beheading her.

"Oh, my god!" cried William.

They watched in horror as the man raised the ax and chopped the rest of her body into pieces.

"This can't be happening!" cried out Norris.

Wiping the blood off his face, the man turned to the other woman, who moaned.

"No!" Norris shouted, and rushed out.

"No! Chief, stop!" yelled Kyle.

Before the ax could reach the woman, a shot rang out. A current ran through the man and he fell. Norris turned to Kyle, who stood with his taser.

The woman screamed and attacked Norris. He grabbed her hands, trying to keep her away. He overpowered her and pushed her away. She groaned and retaliated by charging toward Norris. Kyle shot her. She quivered and fell to the ground.

They stood in shock. William stepped forward and checked their pulses.

"They are alive," he confirmed.

"How long does this work?" Fredrick asked.

"Half an hour, give or take."

"Well, let's make sure they sleep longer." William said.

After sedating, they locked the two people in separate rooms in the basement. They returned to the study and stood silently.

"We need a plan," said William.

They heard screams from a distance. Then a wail.

"It has started," Fredrick said, moving to a corner.

"I have something," Jack called out.

Everyone turned to the screen.

"Two signals have vanished. What did you guys do?"

"We stunned two people," replied Norris.

"With tasers?"

"Yes. What are you thinking?"

"The electrical current emitted by a taser is around 50,000 volts and it might have disabled the nanobots."

"That's doable," William said.

"We don't have that many tasers," Kyle pointed out.

"And we can't go running around shooting everyone. There are just five of us," Norris said.

"Hold on. I have an idea, but it's crazy," William said.

"Crazy will do," Norris replied.

"Okay. And we will need Roumoult and Tom," William added.

39

HOLES IN OUR HEARTS

16th February 2020 (Present day)
Nightridge

illers surrounded them. He didn't know how many villagers were already dead. William held the crying children close to his chest, with his eyes fixed on the forest. The whizzing heightened. The red light became rays that cut through the darkness of the woods. Jack had done it. They were active. The drones were coming.

"William!" Tom yelled. "We have to get out of here!"

William couldn't think of a way out. The drones couldn't differentiate between them and the villagers. If they didn't move fast, they would become targets.

Tom raised his gun toward the villagers. A loud engine killed the silence, and William spun. Two sharp beams of yellow light cut through the darkness, and a truck leaped out. It was the sheriff. Cries erupted around them. A strong spray of water pushed the crowd away from the truck. Kyle swung the fire hose toward the villagers, keeping them away. Villagers from the other side stormed in their direction. The truck came to a halt, and William raced toward it.

"Get in! Get in!" Norris shouted.

William was the first to jump in with the kids. The mob headed straight for them.

"Kyle!" yelled Tom, firing a two warning shots. The mob stopped for a second, but then charged toward them. Throwing the hose away, Kyle jumped in. Norris floored the accelerator. William shielded the children as the creatures moved in their direction.

Tom and Kyle fired at the villagers, but it was useless. They piled over the truck, blocking Norris's view. As the truck lost speed, the children wailed in terror. Horrid faces with black eyes howled. They pounded on the windows, and axes cracked through the roof. William moved away from the window as it cracked and broke. A man grabbed the children, and William hit him in the face. Another pair of hands clutched him. Suddenly they heard whooshing and the man's eyes became still. His face paled, and with a groan, he tumbled. The truck gained speed while an army of drones flew over the Town Center.

"We have to get out of here fast!" William yelled, glancing behind.

A stream of tasers flew down from the sky, targeting the villagers. Screams filled the air. William watched in as their villagers convulsed and crashed to the ground. Although his plan was working, his heart filled with guilt.

As they drove toward safety, sweat and tears covered William's face. But when he looked at the two pairs of grateful eyes, he forgot his pain. The children put their arms around him and didn't let him go. William thought he had done something good. Although, the price was steep.

Mayor's House

Once inside, William rushed to the basement and left the two children with Ms. Pritchard.

"What's going on?" she asked. "Is it working?"

"Yes. Just a few more hours."

"My mom is out there. Did you see her?" asked a little girl.

William had no answer. "I don't know. But if you wait, I promise I'll find her."

He returned to the study. Norris and Tom were watching the front of the house through the windows.

"It's working!" said Fredrick, peering at the screen.

William wasn't proud, but the dots were disappearing. The tasers were deactivating the nanobots. Jack and Roumoult were sharing the other screen. While Jack was busy on the keyboard, controlling the drones, Roumoult was on the phone.

"You can't get there any faster?" he shrieked.

Everyone gathered around the screen.

"Did he finally get help?" asked Tom.

Fredrick turned to Tom. "I think he will…"

"How?"

Fredrick's face turned solemn. "I know you told me not to leave the house. I took a few videos and forwarded it to Cranston, who sent it to the police."

"Good idea," said Tom.

"When!?" Roumoult said, "I understand that Captain, but people are dying!"

The call ended, and Roumoult looked annoyed.

"What happened?"

"After fifteen phone calls, I have finally got someone to agree that this is an emergency."

Norris raises his eyebrows. "And?"

"They will reach Nightridge hopefully in an hour."

"What?!"

"They need to get the squad together, and since there is no bridge, they have to arrange for helicopters. The captain promised he will get there as soon as possible."

"Fine. At least there will be help. Jack, can we stay in control?" Norris asked.

"I don't know…"

"How many drones did you send?"

"We sent out the first fifty to the Town Center. It's clear. The drones took out about two hundred people. Fredrick, we have to be ready to send the next fifty soon."

Fredrick nodded and left the room.

"The problem is, they are scattered all over the area," Jack said.

"Is there a way we can get them together in one place?" asked Norris.

Everyone became thoughtful. Roumoult stood with his arms folded and head bowed. William ran his hand through his hair and paced the room. Everyone was silent.

Roumoult spoke. "I have an idea, but it's insane."

"I think we are well past sanity," said William.

Roumoult appeared distressed. "Are we?"

William sat silently as Fredrick prepared the second wave of drones. All the drones sat on the driveway, small blue lights emitting from their bottom. Like it was magic. The blue lights turned red, and the machines rose from the ground and gained altitude. Like a controlled swarm, they broke up in three groups and headed in different directions.

William's phone rang, and he answered it.

"Are you ready?" said Roumoult.

Sweating, running, and wishing he were somewhere else, William came to a halt. Tom was right behind him.

"I think I don't have to go to the gym for the entire year," he said breathlessly.

William got into the car, and Tom sat in the passenger seat.

"I can't believe we are doing this," Tom said, loading a taser.

"Yep," William replied, and turned the key. The car came to life, and he drove south.

Norris wiped the sweat off his forehead. At least something was working. He didn't like the plan, but it sounded like it might work. They drove toward the north, and he glanced behind at the bag.

"Oh, I don't believe this," Kyle said.

"It's working, Kyle. It's working…"

Kyle's face remained intense. "At what cost?"

Norris had no answer. He had lost too much. He was struggling to save what was left. They all were. He hit the brakes, and Kyle jumped out. Norris watched him run toward his truck and get in. The vehicle came to life and then they drove in separate directions.

William waited in the dark. His phone vibrated, and he saw the picture Fredrick had sent him. The villagers were spread in the woods. He stepped out and picked the two grenades. Had he known his short training in the Navy would come so handy, he would have paid more attention. He hid behind the trees and waited. His phone buzzed again.

In one minute, read the text.

William looked back. The houses behind him looked abandoned. Quiet. A few villagers lay lifeless on the ground. Were they dead or alive? He didn't know and hoped they were still alive. He looked at the phone. Ten seconds remained. He took a deep breath in, pulled the ring off a grenade, and hurled it to his left. The ground shook, and he took cover. Almost simultaneously, more blasts rocked the region. He acted fast and pulled the ring to the second grenade and shoved it in the opposite direction. The forest shook, fire burned through the woods. Getting to his feet, he rushed back toward the truck and got behind the wheel. The blast had attracted the villagers, and the mindless mob appeared from the darkness. He hit the paddle, and the truck rushed ahead. An angry swarm followed him.

Norris's truck was right behind Kyle's. Norris once more looked behind him. The mob charged toward them, blaring and yelling. The forest was on fire. White faces growled at them, coming at them from each direction. Norris tried not to lose control.

William glanced back. Tom was right behind him. They drove over the grass and headed straight to the big clearing. From the north, he saw two more trucks appear. The four trucks converged in the middle of the clearing and stopped. Everyone stepped out and took cover behind the trucks.

Tom stood with William.

"I am sorry," William said.

Tom glanced at him. "For what?"

"For putting you in danger."

Tom eyed him. "Well… if I die today, it will be your fault, and I will haunt you for the rest of your life. So, no apology is necessary."

William couldn't help but smile.

The men waited, armed with tasers. As a backup, he had carried a gun. William realized they might never see the light of day. If the drones failed, he would never see his friends again. He would die before he saw Joan again or his family. He pushed away the negative thoughts and tried to focus. In the fog, he saw shadows that merged as figures. Villagers with torn clothes, hollow eyes shuffled toward them.

"Jack, you better be right about this," Norris spoke into the phone.

"Yes."

Soon they were surrounded. There was no escaping now. This was the last stand.

"Jack?" said Norris.

"Wait for it."

The air was filled with grunts and groans. Just a few paces away, they paused. Faces, dark and hungry, surrounded them. Billy stepped forward, and his eyes set on Norris. They glared at each other. The clearing was full of villagers. William's throat went dry as he stood face to face with the zombies.

"Jack," said Norris.

A loud whizzing filled the air. A big swarm of drones flew over the field.

"Now!" Jack shouted.

Tom, William, Kyle and Norris aimed and fired. The mindless rushed toward them. William shot a man, who jumped over the truck. A sudden cry from behind caught his attention. Two men had grabbed Kyle and were pulling him away. William acted fast and fired. Norris took down the other one. A pair of bloody hands grabbed William and threw him onto the ground. Grabbing William's neck, the mindless creature began strangling and suffocating him.

Norris fired, and the creature convulsed, stumbling over William. William pushed him away and grabbed the stun gun.

The army of drones flew over them, firing at the mob. A few tasers flew past his head. They had to take cover.

"Come on!" Norris yelled, pushing William under the truck.

William checked his stun gun. He was almost out. Norris and Tom tried to control the crowd. Then Norris told Tom to take cover.

A few villagers raised their guns and fired at the drones. A few drones burned and crash to the ground. But they were no match against the flying machines. William covered his ears. Since they had no choice, Tom and Kyle hid under the truck. Norris didn't take cover and kept firing to defend the group.

"Norris!" William yelled.

But the surrounding noise drowned his voice. Something grabbed his leg.

"Ah!" William yelled.

A man started pulling him out. William tried to free himself, but the villager was strong. A shot blasted, and the zombie grunted as blood trickled down his head. The grip around William's leg was released, and he turned to Tom, who shut his eyes in regret.

"Chief!" shouted Kyle.

From the corner of William's eyes, he saw Kyle crawling out. Two men were attacking the sheriff, and one of them was Billy.

Kyle pulled one of them away from him. Norris struck Billy, who was strangling him with his bare arm. William had enough. He crawled out, grabbed his taser, and shot the man who was about to attack Kyle.

A man jumped on him, pushing William to the ground. He tried to free himself, but the villager put grabbed his neck and began choking him. Kyle rushed to his rescue and stunned his attacker.

William caught his breath. Billy and Norris struggled for the gun in the middle of chaos. A loud shot resounded and both men froze.

"No!" William yelled.

The men fell to the ground.

"Norris! Norris!" he cried out, pulling Billy off the

sheriff. William checked his wounds. The sheriff's shirt was smudged with blood, but he was breathing.

William looked at Billy lying on the ground, staring into the abyss. Blood dripped over the grass as breath left him.

William peered over the vehicles and spotted a few villagers trying to escape. The drones flew toward them. Other than that, the field was full of unconscious figures. He held his head. Although the plan had worked, it didn't feel like a victory. He studied the sheriff's face. He was a broken man. Kyle and Tom stood motionless, looking unhappily at the figures on the ground.

Soon, the cries died out, and they heard only the whizzing of the drones. Norris's phone buzzed. At first, he ignored it, but then he answered the call.

"Yes," he said. He turned to William and shut his eyes.

Norris hit the brakes, and armed with stun guns, they stormed toward the swamp.

"I thought we had everyone!" William shouted, preparing his gun.

Tom and Kyle were on their heels.

"It seems there is a group trying to get out of the village. They thought taking the swamp would be a good idea," Norris replied.

The canopy was thick, and the drones navigated ahead of them. In the dark, they heard groans. Norris rushed forward but abruptly stopped when a gun went off. Tom stunned a villager who was walking around nine yards ahead of them.

They rushed down the hill and paused. Kyle raised his weapon and neutralized two people ahead of them.

However, they were too late. Over a dozen men and women had entered the swamp.

"Chief… we cannot use tasers in the swamp. They could get electrocuted," Kyle said, heaving.

"Roger that," Norris replied and jumped into the water and began swam towards the villagers.

"No! Chief," shouted Kyle, following him.

"No! No! The water is contaminated!" shouted William. "Get out. Kyle! Norris!"

Knowing this was a terrible decision, Norris grabbed the older man. Before he could attack him, Norris knocked him out, then grabbed him. He was thankful to see William and Tom on the boat. They grabbed the old man, and Norris swam ahead.

"Norris, get out of the water," William said.

But he wasn't listening. From the corner of his eye, he saw Kyle grab a hysterical woman and was struggling to control her. A gunshot sounded, and he stopped.

"Alligator! There is an alligator in the water! Get out now!" shouted William.

Norris ignored him and continued swimming. The sun was about to rise, and in the dim light he saw heads disappearing underwater.

"No!"

Three villagers came to the surface, yelled for help, but then were pulled under.

"They are trapped," Norris yelled and swam faster.

Again, he heard a burst of gunfire.

Reaching another man, Norris jabbed him and handed him over to William and Tom. Not too far, he caught sight of a familiar face. It was Ethan.

"Ethan! Ethan… stop."

The young man vanished underneath the murky water.

"No!" Norris cried, and dove into the water. He swam as fast as he could. Figures struggled to keep afloat around him. He saw helping hands trying to grab them. Muffled sounds of gunshots were heard. He knew the alligator was nearby, but he wanted to reach Ethan. Not too far ahead, he saw him. He was caught in a web of seaweeds and struggling to breathe. Feeling his own breath grow short, he darted upwards, inhaled deeply, and dove again. He grabbed Ethan and tried to pull him up, but the boy remained trapped. Norris swam downwards and reached for his knife to cut through the weed.

Ethan's body was limp as Norris swam toward the shore.

"Ethan! Ethan!" he called.

Dragging Ethan to the shore, Norris gave him mouth to mouth.

"Ethan, wake up, son! Wake up!"

He placed his palms on his chest and pushed. He put his ear against his chest to listen for a heartbeat. Nothing. He tried again. And again.

"Ethan! Ethan!"

Tears welled up in his eyes, and he saw William working hard to revive an older man. Norris's heart pounded as he stared at Ethan's pale face. There was no pulse, no sign of breath, no movement. He was gone. Tears rolled down his face. Broken, he sat on the damp ground and cried.

40

WHERE DO WE GO FROM HERE?

16th February 2020 (Present day)
Nightridge

Norris remained on the banks of the swamp, along with the bodies lying in a row. Kyle had taken the survivors to the local hospital. Norris gazed at the still water. He had run out of tears, out of hope. A few miles behind him, the whirling sound of helicopters filled the air. Finally, help had arrived. Detective Tom's captain had believed Roumoult and sent a squad, but Norris wished they had come earlier.

The sun shone over their head, and everyone had left except Norris and William. They hadn't said a word, as if each one sat counting their sorrows. The radio buzzed, and Kyle's voice echoed.

"Chief, you need to come to the Town Center."

Norris said nothing. He got to his feet and dusted his

clothes. As they walked toward their vehicle, men in white suits arrived and began picking up the bodies.

Both men silently drove toward the Town Center. As Norris parked the truck, he saw cops everywhere. Villagers with minor injuries were taken to the local hospital. Two helicopters were transferring severely injured villagers to other hospitals. Most of the villagers had gained consciousness and looked lost and frightened.

"Captain Issac," said a man approaching Norris.

Norris shook his hand.

"Sorry about this," the captain said.

Norris said nothing. Sorry wouldn't fix anything. One word couldn't mend a shattered world.

"We will help as much as we can. A small group of doctors are on their way."

Norris just nodded.

"We need to extract the nanobots and send them to the FBI."

Norris didn't care.

"Why?" William said, "its intellectual property."

"Stolen intellectual property which was used as a murder weapon."

"How many casualties?" Norris asked, feeling the hole in his heart widening.

The captain hung his head "Over two hundred."

Norris shut his eyes.

Three Weeks Later
Nightridge

Norris still felt the chilly water of the swamp on his

skin. He had tested positive for mercury poisoning and was taking treatment for the same. He wondered how to get rid of the emotional poison.

When he thought of the dreadful night, still felt his heart race. The drones with stun guns had done less damage than the villagers themselves. Help had arrived, but it was too late. The fires were out, and for the last three weeks men and women wearing uniforms dominated the streets. People had come back to their senses. They had vague memories of what had happened. They felt as if they were drugged or were living a nightmare. For Norris, it was a nightmare that wasn't sure if he would survive.

A group of doctors arrived by helicopter to remove the nanobots. It was a long and arduous process. William assisted the surgeons and skillfully removed the nanobots. The mayor and Hector were arrested for their crimes and would pay a heavy price. But would it be enough?

In the cemetery, Norris stood with several people who mourned the death of their loved ones. Villagers were scattered around the graveyard. The pandemic and the political climate still threatened the peace of his country, but none of that bothered him. He felt dead inside and knew he had failed miserably. This village was his family, and he had lost a lot. Fifty people had been hospitalized, hundreds bruised, hurt, and traumatized. Two hundred villagers were dead. Faces of the villagers who drowned in the swamp haunted him. And Ethan was gone forever.

A silent sob distracted him; it was Ethan's mother. She stood beside him, looking at the grave. Losing a child is difficult for a parent. He had already lost two. He never had a chance to bury his own—his son's and grandson's ashes still waited for his last goodbye. At least Ethan's mom had the chance to meet her son before saying goodbye. Norris wasn't even that lucky.

He stepped forward and put his hand on her shoulder. "I am so sorry…"

Mrs. Lark glared at him. Her eyes were red, swollen, and full of despair. "Why him? Why didn't you save him?"

He knew how she felt. The faces of his dead son and grandson flashed in front of his eyes. Guilt filled his heart, and he gulped hard. "I tried. I tried my best. But I couldn't. I will always regret that."

He stood with the villagers as each of them said their goodbyes. As the sunset, he turned and found Mrs. Flores looking at him with regret.

"Hey, how are you?" he asked.

Tears flowed down her face. "I hurt you… didn't I?"

He didn't let her continue and hugged her.

"I am so sorry," she said, weeping, "I am so sorry."

"It wasn't your fault."

They parted and walked out the cemetery.

"Everyone is thinking of leaving the village…" she said.

Norris hung his head. "I don't blame them."

She turned to him. "What about you?"

Norris stopped. The last twenty-four hours had been dreadful, and everything he held dear was threatened. A part of him wanted to leave, go away, try to forget it. He looked up at the sky and said, "I can't leave. Not now. Not after this."

Mrs. Flores beamed and put her arm around his waist. "I am so glad."

New York

William stood staring at the city lights. The noises on the street were subdued due to the glass. He sipped his whiskey, relishing its taste. The last three weeks had not been easy. William had to quarantine, and Joan had moved to back to her place, leaving him alone. Joan had decided to move out before he had left Nightridge. She had called him to inform him and he didn't want to stop her, and she sensed it. He loved her, but was he ready to have her in his life?

"Where do you think this is going?" he had asked on the phone.

The answer didn't come quickly. Finally, she said, "I don't know. We are too different."

The conversation ended, and they agreed to stay apart for a while. Their relationship was in limbo. One thing he knew, he enjoyed being alone in his apartment, having his own space for now.

The clock chimed 8 pm, and he knew it was time for a social call. He turned on his computer and logged on. It was customary for Roumoult, Jack, and Tom to have drinks after a case. Since they couldn't meet face to face, they met up online. The screen came to life, and he saw Roumoult waiting with a drink.

"Hey... how are you?"

"Not too bad," William said, wondering how to tell Roumoult about Joan.

"So, have you recovered? How are you feeling?"

"Yeah, I am fine," William replied.

He had seen many dead bodies in his lifetime, but the people they couldn't save from the swamp bothered him the most. What frustrated him most was that a bureaucratic ass thought he had the right to take away innocent lives.

"He got bail, you know."

"Not for long. As far as I know, Tom is bringing in the big guns." Roumoult said.

William smiled. "Let's hope for the best."

"And you know Cunningham. He doesn't let go."

William nodded.

"Where is Joan?" Roumoult asked, looking around.

William finished his drink, got up, and brought the bottle of the whiskey. As he filled his glass, he told Roumoult what had happened.

Roumoult's face turned grave. "Okay. Okay. Maybe, we could find you someone else."

"Roumoult…"

"I thought Juliet's friend, Karen, was pretty nice. I think she is a teacher."

"A lecturer." William corrected him, "Roumoult, we aren't exactly… separated."

"You are not?"

"No. We are just taking a break."

Roumoult finished his drink and poured another one. "Maybe you can get a dog!"

William felt like laughing. "I'll be fine."

"Or a cat."

"Roumoult, I want to be alone."

"You have never been alone!"

Roumoult was right. He had never been alone; he was always either in a relationship or getting out of one. For once in his life, he just wanted to be alone. "I think it's about time I am. I'll be fine."

Roumoult's face turned solemn.

The screen blinked, and two faces appeared. It was Tom and Jack.

"How is everyone doing this evening?" Tom asked.

The men raised their glasses, greeted each other, and sipped their drinks.

"Tell me that bastard is going to pay," William said.

"The NYPD and FBI are turning his entire business up and down. He is on bail, he is not going anywhere. They have seized his bank accounts, taken away his passport, and from what I hear, his trial is about to start soon. The press is not leaving him alone. Finally, they have something else to print except the pandemic. Also, they are mad because he was involved in the murder of a journalist. He'll face justice one way or another. Even if he doesn't end up in jail, his entire life will be ruined."

"What about Hector?"

"Oh, he will rot in jail, facing the consequences of his actions."

"Would that be enough?" Roumoult asked. "I want them hanged."

Roumoult's comment didn't surprise William.

"You know, we don't do that anymore...."

"Too bad. Some people deserve it."

"What about the body in the mountain lab?" William asked.

"We got a DNA match. He was the scientist, Dr. Walker, who had developed the nanobots for Sanders."

"Why did he help that lunatic?" asked Roumoult.

"Well... two theories, money, or blackmail," Tom answered. "I spoke with Sanders. He told me that Dr. Walker was eager to further develop his technology. But after the poor media and the pushback, Sanders wanted to stop the project. Henry wanted revenge; he could have paid Dr. Walker enough to advance the technology. But when Dr. Walker found out what his research was being used for, he killed himself."

Roumoult shook his head. "Did you find the nurse who injected the nanobots?"

"Not yet. Her trial is cold. She could be anywhere."

Roumoult frowned.

"Don't worry, we will find her."

"Thank you, Tom," William said.

Jack joined them with a beer in his hand.

"Sorry guys, I am a bit late."

"No problem,"

"Finally, I got my hands on that computer."

William pouted.

"Tell me, how did these nanobots work?" Roumoult asked, leaning forward.

"From what I can understand, they emitted a certain frequency to stimulate the brain. At first, it increased fear and anxiety. No one paid any attention—why? Well, we are in a pandemic. Everyone is a bit over the edge. Then it goes to the next level. The brain is further stimulated to feel anger mixed with fear and paranoia."

William remembered the incident at the town hall.

"The third and the last stage caused the disaster. They lost all control, became violent, crazy, and mindless, just like zombies!"

William wished he used a different word. He had nightmares and woke up in the middle of the night sweating. Currently, he was on sleeping pills.

"How were they activated?" Roumoult asked.

"Each nanobot has a transponder, which was used to track and activate it. The thing is, no one could have controlled them. Henry might have thought he could, but he couldn't. Once the last stage was triggered, there was no stopping it."

"Wow," William muttered, "I am glad we stopped it when we did."

They savored their drinks in silence.

"I miss the days when we could drink together at a pub," Tom pointed out.

Everyone made faces.

"I hope we can do that soon," Roumoult said.

William didn't think that would happen soon. To his surprise, another face appeared.

"Angelus?" the four men said in unison.

"Hey, guys!"

"Where have you been?" William demanded. He could have certainly used Angelus's help in this matter.

"Mexico," said Angelus excitedly. "I was helping a friend solve his brother's murder."

Angelus was a private investigator. He was a well-built man in his mid-forties, tall, with a firm jaw. People trusted him with their deepest secrets and had several clients spread all over the country.

"I hope everything went well," William said, knowing that Angelus wouldn't reveal any details, even if he asked.

"It was all good in the end," replied Angelus.

"Glad you could join us," said Jack, raising his glass.

They sipped their drinks in silence.

"Guys, I need to talk with you about something," Angelus said.

Everyone became alert.

"I think I have an exciting case for us."

William raised his eyebrows.

"I think nothing could top a zombie apocalypse," Roumoult stated blandly.

Angelus eyed him. Clearly thinking Roumoult was joking, he carried on. "My friend told me that two deaths baffled the Mexico police. The victims were found with several bite marks, mostly around their necks. Their blood was drained, and a wooden cross forced through their hearts."

"Oh... no. We are not doing this again," Tom mumbled.

Everyone snickered.

"Vampires?" William chuckled.

"Occult?" Jack speculated.

"Mummification?" Angelus suggested.

"Na... I'll stick with vampires," William said.

Roumoult looked thoughtful. "I can't go to Mexico. Hell, I can't even go home," he muttered.

"I have no jurisdiction in Mexico," joked Tom.

William rolled his eyes. "I just came back, so I don't think I can leave."

Angelus was far too serious. "I began looking for

similar unusual deaths around the country. Over the last one year, there have been several similar murders."

"You have got to be kidding me!" William said.

Angelus picked up a file. "There were two murders in Louisiana and Hayneville, Alabama. Then there were three more homicides in South Carolina and then one in Philadelphia."

"He is moving northeast," noted Roumoult.

"Yes. The last reported murder was in Freehold Township."

"That's close to New York," William replied, placing his glass on the table and rushing to his bookcase. He grabbed an Atlas and returned to the desk.

"I know. I know," Angelus said.

"We have to check it out!" Roumoult said eagerly.

"I hope you guys remember... there is a pandemic. We can't investigate a case. We are in lockdown," said Tom.

"When did the last murder take place?" Roumoult asked.

"Five weeks ago," Angelus replied.

"And here I thought I could have a nice, peaceful drink with my friends," remarked Tom.

"Yeah, me too. Guys, there is a pandemic." Jack insisted.

"If we don't act now, we might lose the trail," Roumoult stated, clearly not listening.

Unfortunately, William was ahead of him. "We need to check out the autopsy reports and need to go through the evidence the police collected. Tom, can you contact them?"

"Hold it. I don't remember saying yes," complained Tom.

"Oh, come on. Aren't you curious?" said Roumoult.

Tom's face turned pensive. He finished his drink. "Don't get me wrong, it's exciting working with you guys. But one day, I am going to get fired, shot, or end up in a looney bin and it's going to be your fault!"

The End

ABOUT THE AUTHOR

H.G. Ahedi holds a PhD in biomedical sciences and is a fictional writer. Reading is one of her favorite hobbies, and she loves watching movies and series while sipping tea. She spends a lot of time writing, and when she is bored with her desk, she wants to hop on a plane and travel the world. As that is not always possible, she explores local Sydney beaches and parks and enjoys a nice cup of coffee.

To join her readers list to get the latest updates, juicy details about her books and free books just click here!

A NOTE TO READERS

Enjoyed *Shadow Pandemic*? Please leave a review and share your thoughts about the book. I would really appreciate it and thank you in advance!

ACKNOWLEDGMENTS

A special thanks to these people for making this book possible.

I would like to thank Shwetha D'souza for her excellent insight and proof reading Shadow Pandemic.
Rebecca, my cover designer is a fine lady who gives power to my imagination.
I would like to thank all my friends on twitter for supporting this book.
Most of all, I would like to thank my family for believing in my dreams and helping me in this journey.

ALSO BY H.G. AHEDI

When Roumoult Cranston drives to Newburgh, a hired assassin awaits him. While trying to unearth this mystery, he discovers a darkness within himself and could be hanged for murder.

Written in the style of Sir Arthur Conan Doyle, you find yourself enthralled!

When three men commit suicides without reason, the hunt for answers become a frantic race against time. If you are interested in gripping crime thrillers, you should read Haunted.

An Engrossing, Brilliant Plot!

Suspenseful Keeps you guessing until the last page!

CALCULATED MURDER

H.G. AHEDI

If you love scandals, secrets affairs with explosive consequences then you should read, Calculated Murder.

Compelling and well-crafted mystery
Caught in the mysterious plot. The details and the accuracy. A great mystery novel

A soldier trying to survive, a scientist trying to save his world and a dark force that will define them both. Transcendence is a historical sci fi novella that will keep you at the edge of your seat.

⋆⋆⋆⋆⋆ H.G. Ahedi's Transcendence is a bit like an episode of "The Twilight Zone" or a macabre, suspenseful nightmare.

Also an Audiobook

Fall of Titan (Realm Book 1) is action packed, mind bending Science Fiction adventure which is a blend of science, archaeology and magic. Imagine Lord of the Rings, just in space.

⭐⭐⭐⭐⭐ Great read! This book has everything I love in scifi: action, splendid world-building, and aliens. Fans of A. G. Riddle, Michael Crichton, and The Expanse will love this book!

Poseidon (Realm book 2): After the fall all is left is blood and revenge.

In the sequel to Fall of Titan... The wrath of the Orias queen has taken everything from Emmeline Augury. Powerless and hunted by the Orias , Emmeline decides not to yield and vows to kill the queen. But she's facing a being as powerful as the gods themselves. Can Emmeline destroy the queen or will the queen triumph? The answers lie in the wake of the Poseidon.

⭐⭐⭐⭐⭐ An Intriguing Plot ⭐⭐⭐⭐⭐ Taut Continuation of the Realm Saga ⭐⭐⭐⭐⭐ Intense sequel